WAR
BONNET

Don Bendell

*The Tenth Exciting Western
in the Chris Colt Chief of Scouts Series*

Ⓢ
A SIGNET BOOK

SIGNET
Published by New American Library, a division of
Penguin Putnam Inc., 375 Hudson Street,
New York, New York 10014, U.S.A.
Penguin Books Ltd, 27 Wrights Lane,
London W8 5TZ, England
Penguin Books Australia Ltd, Ringwood,
Victoria, Australia
Penguin Books Canada Ltd, 10 Alcorn Avenue,
Toronto, Ontario, Canada M4V 3B2
Penguin Books (N.Z.) Ltd, 182–190 Wairau Road,
Auckland 10, New Zealand

Penguin Books Ltd, Registered Offices:
Harmondsworth, Middlesex, England

First published by Signet, an imprint of New American Library,
a division of Penguin Putnam Inc.

First Printing, January 2000
10 9 8 7 6 5 4 3 2 1

This book is dedicated to Jolene Tilley, Dan Naylor, Mark and Carmen Lippincott, Ben Tilley, Peggy Post-lewaite, and all the other family members of the three unfortunate victims of a late-spring storm in the mountains near here in 1998: Troy Tilley, his stepson Drew Naylor, and his buddy Josef Lippincott.

The book is also dedicated to their memory. It is also dedicated to Sue Claxton and her children and the other surviving members of Cortez Colorado Police officer Dale Claxton, who was gunned down this past year by three cruel and unthinking men who took refuge in the desert on the giant Navajo Indian Reservation in southeastern Utah. The tragic legacy of these four is part of the history of the giant mountains and massive deserts, which can be as cruel and unforgiving as they are beautiful and majestic.

The search for the three missing neighbors, and the outrageous cop-killers, however, showed how many people can be unselfish and caring of others, and reminds us of what is truly important in life. I also dedicate this book to you, one and all, friend and foe alike, who took part in those searches. May we all work to make their untimely deaths meaningful to society. For in the end, we must always remember that we all live together on our one little spot in the universe and no man or woman can exist, completely and happily, alone. We never know when each of us will be called away, but at some point, each of us will.

In God's love,

Don Bendell

ACKNOWLEDGMENTS

I never thought I would find a horse that could replace Hawk, my magnificent big Appaloosa that saved my life several times in the very mountains where Chris Colt rides. He won me a few match races, and even a trophy for All-Around Cowboy at a ranch rodeo. I have, however, found another friend who seems to be another one of those once-in-a-lifetime horses. Chris Colt's horse War Bonnet is patterned after my magnificent, sixteen hands tall, black-and-white pinto gelding Eagle. Eagle has shown that he has more heart than ten horses, and he is classy, too. Half Arabian and half American Saddlebred, he is proud and majestic, and can go all day in the rugged mountain terrain. Eagle can gallop over terrain that makes mules shiver and balk, and he has absolutely no quit in him. He loves roping cows and has only one speed: fast. I hope and pray we share many more years of friendship and adventure together.

Chris Colt's pet wolf, Kuli, was created after my own one hundred and fifty-plus pound pet wolf, Kuli. Half tundra wolf, one-sixteenth Husky, and seven-sixteenths timber wolf, Kuli was simply the best pet I ever had. The stories about him are numerous and colorful. His last adventure and the last time I saw him before his death was when he accompanied my wife, our horses, and me up on a lonely mountaintop to search for a missing hiker. Kuli knew he was on an important mission and a great adventure. He is now buried near the "Prayer Rock," and will always be missed and remembered fondly by our family.

—Don Bendell

Our Heroes

I feel like I'm a normal guy
They treat me strange, so tell me why.
I always try to do what's right.
But it doesn't mean I don't feel fright.

I do feel fear, and I do get scared.
That time was just because I cared.
I might get hurt or maybe die,
But I just can't sit idly by.

Why do they all say I'm so brave?
That day quite simply was very grave.
I'm sure that others would do like me.
But not to make folks jump with glee,

Then shake my hand and slap my back,
And then tell me that I have a knack
To be a hero and make them proud,
"Now say a word to our grateful crowd."

For I believe that fear is strong,
But I cannot do what is wrong,
I simply just do what I can.
I'm not a hero, just a man.

By Don Bendell from *Of Doves, Hawks, and Eagles,*
the collected poems of Don Bendell (1998, Don Bendell, Inc.)

"There is no secret so close as that between a rider and his horse."

—R. S. Surtees (1803–1864)

WAR BONNET

BACKGROUND:
THE COLT FAMILY

Chris Colt became famous as a chief of scouts for the U.S. Cavalry and was equally famous for his iron nerve and the speed and deadliness of his quick draw. Born to a cobbler in Cuyahoga Falls, Ohio, and related to the famous Colonel Samuel Colt, young Chris would visit Uncle Samuel, entranced by the gunsmiths at the famous factory back East. He started practicing quick draw secretly as a boy, and pining for adventure and excitement, he joined the 171st Regiment of the Ohio National Guard as a teenager and went off to fight for the Union Army in the Civil War. Chris became a scout and started learning about courage, and developed tremendous stalking and tracking skills. Ohio held nothing for him after the war, and he journeyed west where he worked at many jobs before scouting for the cavalry. His abilities and reputation grew rapidly with each adventure, and he was soon a chief of scouts.

He also fell in love with a Minniconjou Lakotah (Sioux) woman named Chantapeta, for Fire Heart, and they had a little girl named Winona, for First Born. Both were raped and murdered by four renegade Crow warriors, and the brokenhearted chief of scouts hunted down and killed each one.

Hired as chief of scouts for George Armstrong Custer, whom he could not stand, Chris Colt was befriended by the famous Lakotah warrior/ chieftain Crazy Horse. Fired by Custer on the way to the Little Big Horn, Chris Colt was held and bound by Crazy Horse in the giant encampment during the Battle of the Little Big Horn, so he would not warn Custer or fight against the Lakotah, Cheyenne, and Arapaho. Sitting Bull had wisely warned Colt that he could never tell of his presence at the battleground or people would think he deserted Custer. At the same time, Crazy Horse had rescued the woman Colt fell in love with, Shirley Ebert of Bismarck, Dakota Territory, who had been kidnapped by a giant of a man named Will Sawyer.

Chris Colt later hunted the man down, killing him in a fight in the Valley of the Yellowstone.

He married Shirley, and they had two children, Joseph and Brenna, who were raised on Colt's ranch, the Coyote Run. Shirley, ironically, had grown up in Youngstown, Ohio, not too far from Cuyahoga Falls. Chris and Shirley shared the sprawling ranch at the base of the Sangre de Cristo Mountains in the Wet Mountain Valley in southern Colorado, with Chris's older half brother, Joshua Colt, who was a twin to Chris except for his brown skin and black curly hair. The bastard son of a love union between Chris's dad and a slave, Joshua Colt had forgotten more about the cattle business and horses than most ranchers knew.

Colt ended up with Chief Joseph of the Nez Perce in their 1,700-mile fighting flight for freedom, which is still considered the greatest tactical fighting retreat of all time. It was also the first time that the press and public opinion took the side of the Indians, because Colt persuaded Chief Joseph not to attack civilians or take scalps. The cavalry, on the other hand, took Nez Perce scalps and brutally killed women and children.

Colt and his young Nez Perce sidekick, Man Killer, also led the scouting for the all-black buffalo soldiers in their campaign against the feared Apache renegade leader Victorio.

After that, Chris Colt was made Deputy U.S. Marshal, and deputized Man Killer to work for him. Man Killer married a Westcliffe beauty named Jennifer Banta who had inherited a fortune. Chris Colt's reputation and legend grew even larger as a deputy sheriff, as did Man Killer's, especially when the young brave went so far as to have himself purposely shanghaied so he could sail to Australia to rescue his Jennifer, who had been taken off by a greedy uncle.

Also growing in reputation down in Texas was Chris Colt's younger cousin, Justis Colt, who was becoming famous as a Texas Ranger. He was always escorted by his mute Comanche-trained sidekick, Tora, a former Samurai warrior from Japan.

Now another Colt had sprung up—Chris and Joshua's ravishing younger sister, Charley Colt, who was another love-child of their father and a beautiful southern aristocrat. Charlotte Colt only learned at her mother's deathbed that she was indeed the love-child of her mother and the father of Chris and Joshua Colt. She married a man named James Adams who had been murdered by his assistants on his freight operation, which secretly carried gold for the U.S. government. The head turncoat, Drago Meconi, still had that gold, and Charley Colt had been working jobs dressed as a man so she could support her two little girls. At the same time, she had been hunting down the men who betrayed and killed her husband.

Charley finally had a shoot-out with the men, her brothers finally learning her identity and helping her to kill the man who murdered her husband. Chris and Joshua took her and her two daughters in, and she became part of their ranch, their fortune, and more important, their family.

Some of the lowest life forms to ever operate in the West decided to try to kidnap the four children of Charlotte, Chris, and Shirley. In their attempt, Shirley Colt sacrificed her own life to hold them at bay while the children fled into the mountains. The four kids outwitted the killers over and over, while Chris and Charley pursued them, eventually saving them.

Chris then went on a campaign to avenge his wife's death and ended up being shot to doll rags, surviving an entire winter in a thicket on the prairie in Kansas. Healing his own wounds, and having no weapons, clothes, food, matches, or horse, he survived by just his wits and determination. All the men were brought to justice, usually at the business end of a Colt gun, but in the process Chris Colt had to question his own dedication to law and order and principle.

CHAPTER 1
Manhood

The streets of Silver Cliff were muddy with the late spring thaw, and Brenna Colt carefully picked and chose the little dry islands of hard-pack to hop onto while carefully holding up the folds of her gingham dress. Her older brother, Joseph, like their giant father Chris Colt, ignored the puddles and plowed straight ahead, their eyes on the Emporium, where the promised ice cream would soon be enjoyed. The male Colts were serious eaters of anything sweet, and this was important business, very important business indeed.

Chris Colt was a resplendent figure of a frontier man. Standing taller than most other men in any setting, he had a rugged handsomeness, and an ever-present smile in the corners of his hazel eyes that made it look like he had the answer to some secret that all would like to know.

Wearing a quilled, fringed, and beaded buckskin Lakotah war shirt, his waistline was cinched by a gun belt holding two Colt .45 Peacemakers with hand-carved ivory handles, each with the Mexican emblem of a bald eagle clutching a large rattlesnake in its talons. Behind the right-hand gun hung a very large beaded and fringed sheath, which held a razor-sharp Bowie knife with an elk antler handle. His old faded cavalry trousers were tucked into high-top black boots with riding heels, each decorated with large roweled Mexican spurs and tiny bells on the outside. Over his sandy hair was a leather scout's hat with a single eagle feather attached to the hatband. The sun reflected brightly off the star over his left breast, its letters were clearly visible in the afternoon sun; "Deputy U.S. Marshal." The rippling muscles and sinew that came from years of hard work could not be disguised under any of his clothes.

Joseph looked like a miniature version of his famous father, while Brenna favored her late mother, right down to the long, beautiful auburn hair. She was a gorgeous six-year-old, and it was easy to see that she would become a very beautiful woman when full grown.

The three had ridden into town early in the morning and had been shopping and just spending the day together, something Chris Colt made sure he did with his two children as often as possible after the tragic murder of his wife, Shirley. They would eat their ice cream, then make the ten-mile ride north to their ranch, the Coyote Run, at the base of the Colorado Sangre de Cristo mountain range in the beautiful Wet Mountain Valley.

The Emporium sign was inviting Joseph forward with each step, and even his right foot sinking calf deep into a mud puddle was barely noticed in his quest for a sweet cold treat. Aunt Charley was a very good cook, but she could not make the apple or sweet potato pies that Joseph's ma had been able to serve up, and he really missed the sweets.

But now Joseph did notice something was wrong, and he immediately went into action. A young man dressed in black boots, black trousers, a black ruffled shirt, and a black leather vest, wearing a gray Stetson hat, and oddly enough, a green silk scarf wrapped and tied about his neck, appeared in the street before them. He also sported a pair of pearl-handled Colt .44 Russians in shiny black silver-studded holsters. His clothes and boots were spotless, but none of his finery could disguise the ugliness of his young visage, which reminded Joseph of the sharp-toothed face of an opossum. The man had a long pointy nose and crooked upper teeth that protruded slightly down through his closed lips. His dark eyes were very deep-set. A small cigarette dangled from his thin lips.

Chris Colt was already sizing the man up when he walked out the door of the saloon. The first thing the lawman noticed were the three notches carved into the handle of each six-shooter. He had seen young strutting peacocks like this before, and worried that there would be trouble. He also noticed that the Russian .44s' barrels did not protrude through the bottom of the youth's short black holsters. It was his guess that the man was Johnny "Little Guns" Oxendine, originally from the Pembroke area of southeastern North Carolina. Johnny got his nickname because he felt he could draw faster if his barrels were shorter, so he sawed them off. Half Lumbee Indian himself, he had been hanging out in the Indian Territory, trying to establish a reputation as a shootist.

The lawman and his children walked faster, passing the saloon without looking over at the young tough.

As soon as he sarcastically yelled, "Hey U.S.

Marshal Chris Colt! Turn around, will ya!" Joseph knew what to do.

He grabbed his sister by the hand and quickly led her away from his father as fast as he could move. Christ felt good, knowing that his son had so much sense, but his own senses now had to be as sharp as ever.

He watched to see if the young man was staggering or wobbly-kneed at all, assuming he had consumed at least some liquor to work up his courage. He wasn't.

Johnny said, "You know who I am, Colt?"

Chris smiled and said calmly, "I really don't care, sir. I just want to go buy my children some ice cream. I'll be on my way, if you don't mind."

"I mind!" Little Guns yelled. "Yer supposed to be fast and killed all kinds of men, but I saw you shooting up in Cheyenne, and I think I can take you."

The hardcase stepped out into the street.

Colt said, "If you think you can, you're probably right. Being able to shoot faster or straighter than me is not something to be known for. Why don't you try to become a big rancher, a famous scout, a lawyer, a preacher, a successful merchant? Those are the things that are better to become known for."

"Naw," the persistent killer said, "I'm gonna be the man that beat and killed Chris Colt!"

The last thing that Colt wanted to do was have to bury another idiot, especially having to shoot him down in front of his children. He did know one thing by looking at the man's clothing and shiny boots: He would not want to look bad, even if Colt did kill him. Chris thought maybe there was some way he could turn the killer around, or at least change the man's goals in life. Chris moved to a freighter wagon parked along the boardwalk, ten feet to his right. As the gun stiff's hand hovered over his right gun, Colt reached in the floorboard of the wagon and grabbed the small box of stones that the driver kept there to throw at the mule's rumps when he wanted them to move.

Joseph held Brenna back and crouched in a doorway with a barber and two customers standing over them, all watching the gunfight unfold.

Everyone, including Johnny Little Guns, was puzzled as the famous lawman walked toward the young gunfighter, the small wooden box clutched under his left arm. Colt's lips tightened into an angry scowl.

Johnny commanded, "Stop right there, Colt,

and don't come any closer." His hand almost trembled, and he was ready to draw.

Angrily, Colt snarled, "So you're a big tough gunfighter, huh?"

Chris, at the same time, reached into the box and pulled out a stone and threw it as hard as he could at the gunfighter. It hit Johnny in the left thigh and made him wince and howl in pain.

Colt kept walking fast as he grabbed another stone and threw, saying, "You want to be the man who killed Chris Colt, huh," and he threw another, each time making the want-to-be killer duck and cover his face with his arms.

Still walking forward and throwing stones, Colt growled, "I've seen a hundred strutting young turkeys like you and seen hundreds buried just the same. Each one thought they were the best, and couldn't believe it when they died. Now, you're going to learn a lesson about manhood, son."

The young man was so shocked and unnerved by Colt's decisive and unexpected actions that he didn't even try to draw his guns. He just tried to dodge and block the bruising lumps he was receiving from the stones. Colt was almost upon him, and the numerous gathered towns-people not only roared with laughter, but started cheering and applauding Colt as well. Colt made it right up to the gunfighter and dropping the box of stones, he jerked the man forward by both lapels. He reached down with his right hand and yanked out one of Johnny's guns, then the other, tossing them into the dust of the street.

Johnny was not only shocked, he was totally embarrassed now. Colt help him by one lapel and slapped his face from one side to the other, as the man tried to raise his forearms to ward off the blows. Colt then literally picked the man up with both hands and held him high overhead, walking over to a nearby watering trough, where he unceremoniously tossed him into the water.

He then yanked Johnny right out and sent the sputtering young man sprawling across the street as the entire population of the town, it seemed, gathered around. When Johnny tried to rise, Colt shoved him facedown into the dust with his foot.

Colt said quietly, "You wouldn't have dressed like that and spent so much time shining your boots and wearing that fancy green scarf if you didn't want people to notice you. Anyway, now they've noticed you. Still want to be a gunfighter?"

The man just looked down at the ground in shame.

Colt went on, "Make something of yourself and people will notice you and respect you. Being fast with a gun, sonny, is not something to be famous for. Any fool can learn a fast draw. Only a real man can learn how to live without shooting others. Now, git, and don't ever come back."

Holding his head down in shame, Johnny said nary a word, but got up and ran toward the livery stable while well-wishers came up and clapped Chris Colt on the back and shook his hand.

Joseph and Brenna ran up and hugged each of Colt's legs, as he knelt down saying, "I promised you two an ice cream, didn't I?"

From the upstairs window over the confectionery, the building owner, Daniel Yost, and his friend, Swede Johanson, watched from Yost's offices where he ran his several enterprises. Yost had a coal company, real estate investments, and a small store that sold precious gems and "original Indian artifacts." Swede was his foreman for the coal operation.

Daniel said, "Good for Colt, but I wish he would have hanged the tough. That would get the message to those who want to invade this town."

"Well, boss, the Vigilance Committee could still take care of thet little matter," Swede said.

"Well, if the shootist tries to return, we will," Daniel replied. "I don't think it will occur, however. Marshal Colt got rid of this one for good, I believe. That Colt, though—always sticking his nose into everyone else's business. I do believe the Vigilance Committee would have set a more proper example with that young gun tough."

Swede nodded his head dumbly, grumbling about Colt and troublemakers with the same breath.

Daniel Yost stared out the window at the back of the famous lawman. The merchant had his own plans and wondered if the lawman would become a hindrance. If Colt did, he decided, he would simply manipulate the Vigilance Committee he formed to solve problems for him. Besides, a man who thought he took care of every detail, Yost had already made plans for Colt, plans to back up the one that failed.

Down in the street, Joseph looked up at his father. "Pa?"

Chris looked down, saying, "What, son?"

"I sure am proud to have the name Colt," Joseph said.

Chris cleared his throat and tousled his son's hair, saying, "Come on. I need some ice cream."

Brenna grabbed her father's big hand and started skipping. "Pa, this is fun. Do you have to leave again and shoot more bad men?" she said.

Colt tried hard to force a smile and patted her on the head. Would that ever end? he wondered.

Just than, a telegrapher with black garters on his sleeves and a shaded brim crownless cap on his head ran up. "Marshal Colt! Important telegram for you, sir!"

Chris gave him a tip and read the paper he was given. He frowned and looked at his little children. He dropped down and threw his beefy arms around both of them and hugged them.

CHAPTER 2

Wah Pe Can

His copper-colored muscles rippled in the moon-light, and the moon's rays shone even more brightly on the blade as it twisted in his large hand. The warrior grabbed a scoopful of white snow and held it up to his mouth, nibbling on it. It had been unseasonably warm this day, even up here, where you usually looked down and not up to see the clouds. He studied the blade as he turned it one way and then the next. Wah Pe Can grew up in the tribe of Chris Colt's first wife, Chantapeta, the Minniconjou, of the Lakotah nation. He lived, as did the rest of his tribe, on the Red Cloud reservation, but now was living far away in the hills, as he had been banished from the tribe.

Wah Pe Can had committed adultery with the wife of his cousin, which was a wrong and cer-tainly not condoned, but he made it worse when he tried to lie when confronted with his deeds. Her nose was slit as punishment, but he was exiled for lying, something that simply was never done by any Lakotah brave. To brag or boast about one's exploits in battle or hunting was encouraged, but lying was unpardonable. It was unthinkable.

Banishment was so disgraceful and such a tremendous blow to the psyche of Wah Pe Can, or Thunder as the *wasicun* would call him, he literally had a psychotic breakdown. Wah Pe Can would speak normally for a few sentences, then go off into a totally different conversation with some unseen listener. He also would lapse into blank stares that would last for minutes at a time.

Now, completely insane, he was simply sneaking into the lodges of the Minniconjou, usually under the cover of darkness, killing tribal members, usually women and children. His murders were always brutal, and always done with his honed knife. Members of the tribe were getting very upset, and everyone was on edge. All knew that it had to be another Sioux, for a *wasicun* could never sneak in and out of their village and do such a thing.

Wah Pe Can had been watching one young boy in particular, the only son of Shong Ila Mi

Na Shapa, Black Fox, a mighty war chief of the Minniconjou. He was relatively young but had counted many first coups already, and was the youngest to sit among the elders when the pipe was passed. He had become a sundancer before thirty summers had passed, too, and had given up thirty pieces of flesh when he performed the sundance ceremony.

Each day after chores, this young lad would grab his bow and work the brush piles along the river, kicking out small cottontail rabbits. When the rabbit would scamper from the thick brush, the boy would whistle, mimicking the cry of a red-tailed hawk, causing the rabbit to stop and freeze in fear. Then he would unleash his arrow at the small quarry.

It was after watching the boy carefully for two full weeks that Wah Pe Can finally struck, leaving only a part of the remains of the boy for the family to recover. Afterward, nobody wanted to be near Black Fox. The warrior took a blood oath to track down the killer, and send him on a journey on the spirit trail.

He set out the day following his son's death, jaw thrust in defiant silence, eyes affixed on the horizon. The same day, the sister of Chantapeta, first wife of Chris Colt, went to the Red Cloud Agency and convinced a trader there to send a "singing wire" to Chris Colt and let him know about the killer.

Chris Colt was in Canon City by the next morning, and ready to board the first train that would make connections for him to head north.

Several days later, he rode into the village of his former in-laws and was greeted with much warmth. It stirred memories in the lawman's heart, but Chris Colt was not there to visit and reminisce.

That same day, Chris Colt set out on the trail of the Lakotah serial killer. He did not want to waste any more time. He started looking where the little boy was kidnapped and where his body had been found, but there was no real sign. Too much time had elapsed, and Black Fox had already carefully combed both sites, finding one piece of natural buckskin fringe that had caught and pulled off on a fallen log. The piece of leather told him nothing except that the killer was probably Lakotah, but he already assumed that anyway.

Colt simply followed Black Fox's tracks now, for the man had already started working out the trail before him.

Chris figured that it would not take long for him to catch up with the angry father, for War Bonnet, his magnificent paint, the gift from

Crazy Horse, did not like walking. Colt often joked with people that his horse had one speed and that was "full out." War Bonnet was the fastest walking horse Chris Colt had ever been on, and the big gelding always wanted to trot, or better yet, canter, and Colt had to constantly keep the spotted horse in check. Many times, War Bonnet, knowing his master wanted a slower gait, would do a slow trot, sometimes prancing sideways, however, in impatience. But when Chris was tracking someone, War Bonnet seemed to know it and was totally sensitive to the bit and his master's commands.

They headed up into the high ground, and the lodges fell away behind and below them, soon becoming dots out on the high prairie. By morning, Chris Colt found himself where the clouds are born, high up above timberline on a steep-sided ridge that would make most horses cry and quiver in fear. Far below him, as the early shadows quickly gave way to illuminating sunlight, Colt saw the lone figure of Black Fox, kneeling on the ground, inspecting the tracks of the killer. Wah Pe Can was clearly headed downhill, and Colt could see the giant watercourse he was probably headed for. That was one of the biggest parts of true tracking—trying to determine what a person was doing, or would do, by looking at the overall picture, instead of just the tracks. Colt saw that Black Fox was meticulously following just the tracks. From Chris's perch however, he could see the faint outline of the trail going downhill off the glacial field. Seeing the ridges down below that eventually led to the river out on the prairie floor, Colt determined the killer's objective. He would bypass Black Fox and head straightaway for the river.

It was late afternoon, however, when Chris Colt finally unraveled the next part of the trail. The murderer had previously hidden a Lakotah round-bottomed bull-boat made of buffalo hide in the thick brush along the watercourse, and had long since disappeared downstream. Colt would now move at a rapid pace with the big horse and his mile-eating trot and canter. He would have to slow down or stop at every likely place the boat would have stopped, but fortunately for him, most of the stream banks were cut-banks with steep sides, sometimes as high as thirty feet. As Chris Colt moved along the stream, he noticed how thick the greenery was along the watercourse. Colt started thinking about what a good hiding place a stream or river would make. There was water to drink, and game would come there to drink, too. Because of the large amounts of water in the soil, the brush was so thick along most streams and rivers, Colt figured one could hide a whole army in many places. He watched more closely as he rode along the tributary.

Colt kept riding hour after hour, allowing War Bonnet occasional rest breaks, but not very long ones. He saw another stream run off the larger one and wondered if maybe the wily serial killer might have taken the detour. It dropped at a more rapid pace than the other stream, and could afford a faster getaway. On the other hand, the streamside vegetation ended and may not have provided plenty of hiding spots. Colt trotted down the narrow watercourse for a mile but found no broken twigs or leaves torn off any branches hanging over the stream, and finally figured that the killer must have stayed on the main stream. He turned the big paint and headed back uphill toward the stream's junction again.

Colt set out to find sign of the killer down the main waterway; and after just fifteen minutes of searching, finally found two broken twigs where the man's body brushed against low overhanging branches as he floated downstream. Chris had War Bonnet pick up the pace again, stopping sometimes to rest at likely spots where the killer could pull the boat out of the water. It was almost dark when Colt finally found the depression where the round-bottomed bullhide boat had indeed been pulled up on the bank. Wah Pe Can had relieved himself, and ate some jerky. He then got back in the boat and continued downstream.

Colt did not find any other sign until midmorning the following day. This time, however, the tracks were somewhat different. Chris didn't know why at first. The terrain was now much rockier, and this particular place where the boat had been pulled from the stream was at the base of a steep rocky canyon. The man had apparently hidden the boat and slept in the thick brush for a few hours, then put the boat back in the stream and continued on. War Bonnet was the one to alert Colt that he was wrong. As he mounted up and started back down the stream, the horse balked and faced up the rocky canyon.

Colt squeezed his left leg into the big paint's flank and pulled the reins to the right, clucking to the horse.

"Come on, War Bonnet, what's wrong?" he said.

Colt was not used to his horse balking like that, so he knew something was wrong. Chris looked up the canyon, then back at the stream. He dismounted and dropped the reins.

Colt started searching. Before he had looked at the now familiar marks of Wah Pe Can dragging the bullhide boat into the stream. Now, as he got down on his hands and knees, Chris's eyes carefully searched each track and every little drag mark. His skilled eye was looking for the slightest sign, something—anything—out of order.

After an hour of diligent searching, he finally spotted the missing piece of the puzzle. Colt retraced every track and sign the killer made as he left the water, rested, then returned to the watercourse. The lawman finally waded out into the water and, taking care not to muddy the bottom, checked each rock and waterlogged stick on the stream bottom until he found what he was after. Upstream about eight feet from where the killer put the boat in, Colt saw three peculiar small rocks that had been overturned toward the bank. Other stones in the stream were covered with a thin layer of moss and silt, but these three stones had been turned over and were clear. They had rolled toward the shore, which meant that the killer had gotten out of the boat, probably in mid-stream, walked upstream a few steps, and then waded back to the shore, crawling out among the dense bushes. Colt knew he would find faint traces of a trail at the stream's edge, and he did. Looking very closely, he even saw where the killer had carefully tied a stick that had bent over to another stick with a long piece of grass, so that the broken one would appear to be standing upright to any viewers.

Away from the stream's edge, Colt noticed an unusual number of green leaves from cottonwood saplings lying on the ground. Looking up, he saw that the killer had moved toward the gulch by climbing up in a sapling, swinging it back and forth until he could grab the next one uphill, stepping from one high fork to the next and continuing on. Once he figured out how the killer was hiding his steps, the trail stood out like a bawdy girl's best dress. Instead of continuing to check each individual sapling, Colt just went to the mouth of the gulch and found where the serial killer had carefully climbed down from the last sapling and onto the rocks.

As much as some fugitives longed for rocky areas to hide their footsteps, Colt was now glad that the killer was going up the rocky draw. It actually saved Colt hours of tracking, because the steep terrain dictated where the killer would walk. Up closer to the head of the draw, Chris dismounted and searched for sign. He found it almost immediately. The murderer, like anybody in that situation, tried to step from rock to rock, but occasionally a smaller one would overturn or slide out of place, showing dark smudges of earth underneath. That was all the sign that Colt needed to know that he was still hot on the trail of the child slayer.

Chris kept on until he could no longer find any telltale clues, then started backtracking his way down the steep gulch. On the southern side of the gulch was a sheer rock wall that rose about four hundred feet. Its northern side was almost as steep, both sides totally unscalable by man or beast without ropes and other climbing equipment. Chris, knowing that the killer did not go up any farther, knew that he had returned down the gulch, where he surely would have run into Chris; or he had escaped by some unseen route. With this in mind, Colt chose the steeper side on the south wall and started searching for a notch, a crevice, a cave, an old mine, anything that would afford concealment.

Along that wall, and behind a small stand of cedars, Colt found a crack in the rock that went back twenty feet before turning to the left. It was extremely narrow, but he checked it anyway. Ground-reining War Bonnet at the crevice,

Colt squeezed through, unable to carry anything with him as the fit was so tight. In spots, he even had to inhale and hold his breath to pass sideways between the high walls. He saw what he wanted within just five minutes. The killer had covered his tracks, which was fairly easy because the floor of the narrow walkway was mainly rock slab. But as Chris examined both walls, he found a long strand of black hair that had clung to the rock. The sky was suddenly dark as Colt looked up. Overhead, numerous large boulders had fallen into the crack and loomed above like a three-hundred-and-fifty-foot-tall ceiling. Some boulders looked as though a strong breeze would be all it would take to jar them loose and send them crashing down on the scout-turned-lawman.

Colt persisted—especially since the only way he could get out was to squeeze back the way he had come. The killer had continued on—Colt would, too.

Black Fox studied the large paint at the entrance to the narrow opening. The saddlebags and canteen seemed full, and there was a Winchester carbine in the saddle boot. The large horse was shod, and there was a fancy saddle on it, with tapadero teardrop stirrup covers on it, but the horse had eagle feathers braided into its mane and tail, and red coup stripes around each upper foreleg. It looked like a large version of an Indian war pony other than the white man's saddle, bridle, and shoes. The horse was very well muscled and had long straight cannons. His coat, eyes, and build showed that he was very well fed and cared for. Black Fox recognized that this horse could only belong to one man—the famous Wamble Uncha, Chris Colt. No matter, he thought. It was his right and his duty to exact revenge for his son's killer and that he would do.

He tied his own pony to a sapling and turned himself sideways squeezing into the crack, eyes on the ground, looking for tracks.

Chris Colt saw green ahead and wedged forward rapidly when rifle shots suddenly rang out, bullets ricocheting on the rock walls above his head. He could draw only his right-hand gun, and he fired at the flash from the trees now visible up ahead. Another shot rang out, and Colt felt the whip of the bullet past his cheek and pinging off the rock behind him. Colt pushed his way out of the passageway and dived forward, thumbing more rounds into the cylinder of one gun.

As soon as it had started, the shooting stopped.

Colt came up on one knee, his heart pounding in his neck and ears while his eyes scoured the treeline before him for the hidden sniper. Suddenly, Colt realized he was totally exposed to more gunfire, and he ran straight ahead into the trees. Once there, his eyes darted left and right, searching for the unseen shooter. Colt looked down and found the shells from ejected forty-fours. The man had been shooting a carbine like his own. Colt saw where the man had knelt behind a pine tree to fire at him. He now looked around, seeing he was in a hidden box canyon filled with grass and trees, maybe a few hundred acres in size. Tall rock walls surrounded the canyon on every side, and the large stand of trees in which Colt now stood was traversed by a cold spring-fed stream.

A sudden shot clipped Colt's hat off his head, and he quickly hunched down behind a tree, looking out in time to see the sniper, a big Lakotah Indian with a carbine, kneeling behind a large tree. Chris emptied both guns into the tree and on both sides of it as the man ducked back, sticking his head out defiantly from time to time. Colt reached back on his holster and checked his bullet loops, finding only enough ammunition to reload one pistol.

Colt knew he had to get back to War Bonnet and retrieve his Winchester and more bullets. He turned in time to see Black Fox emerging from the crack. Black Fox fired at Colt right away, showering his head with splinters. Colt dropped and swung around the tree again, looking back over his shoulder, seeing that the sniper had used the distraction to take off.

Black Fox kept Colt's head down by emptying his own rifle into the tree over Colt's head.

While he reloaded, he shouted, "Wamble Uncha, go home! My fight is with Wah Pe Can, the man who sent my son on the spirit journey! I am not here to take the scalp of Colt! I am here to kill this man who killed my son! I will take his heart out and eat it! Go away!"

"No! It is my job to arrest him," Colt yelled back. "I am sorry about your son, but I will bring him to justice, my brother! That is my job!"

"You are not my brother! If you stand between Wah Pe Can and me, my bullet shall find your heart!" Black Fox raged.

Colt answered, "Look, we are after the same man for the same reason. We cannot fight against each other. I understand how you feel, but let me handle it!"

Chris thought about the recent murder of his

wife, and the brutal killing of his first wife and daughter. He thought about the revenge he enacted for the deaths and how he almost compromised his loyalty to the law. He truly understood the feelings of Black Fox, but the Sioux warrior wouldn't believe that. He had planned for his son to rise as a great leader among the Lakotah. Maybe someday he would have become the man who could at long last receive the blessings of the Great Spirit and turn back the white tide. Now, the killer in the trees was within Black Fox's grasp, and this *wasicun* stood between them.

Chris knew he had to get past the angry brave to get to his saddlebags and then pursue the killer. Colt retreated farther into the trees and quickly climbed one to survey the box canyon and confirm his initial impression that the crack was the only way in or out. He was also able to see the patch of woods and the wide expanse of green grass all around. Climbing back down, Colt noticed deer tracks everywhere. The only animals coming in or out of this canyon would have to fit through the crack in the sheer rock.

Colt knew that the easy thing to do would be to just stay by the crack and get the killer when he tried to leave, but with all of the shelter, water, and game in this hidden valley, a person could hide here forever. Chris was very angry at himself for leaving his rifle and extra ammunition.

He stayed out of sight in the trees and watched Black Fox. The Minniconjou warrior realized that he, too, was exposed, and he moved into the trees as well. Colt watched as the brave followed the tracks of the serial killer, following his trail deeper into the trees. Once Black Fox was out of sight, Colt headed toward the crack.

Without warning, the ground started shaking violently. Chris Colt became frightened. He looked all around him and tried to figure out what was happening. It finally dawned on him that what he was experiencing was an earthquake. Colt looked at the crack in the rock with a sense of panic as the ground finally ceased to shake. He had heard about the quakes that occurred in California, but to someone who had never been through an earthquake before, it was still a nerve-shattering event.

Among the trees, Black Fox stood and raised his arms to the sky, shouting out a war cry, as he was certain the Great Spirit was letting him know he shared in his anger and thirst for revenge.

Two hundred yards away, Wah Pe Can thought about the men stalking him and how he would kill them both and eat their body parts. His eyes were empty and emotionless as he looked around. He knew that Mother Earth had shaken a great deal, but it meant nothing to him. He now had prey to attack. It would not be as easy for him as the children and women were, but they were prey just the same.

As Chris moved forward, his greatest fears were realized. The giant boulders above the crack had fallen, and what was once a fissure had now been filled in with solid rock. On the other side stood War Bonnet, a magnificent horse fully outfitted with a saddle, saddlebags, rifle in a scabbard, Cheyenne bow and arrows wrapped inside a bedroll, and a bridle. In other words, the unreachable horse was carrying everything his almost bulletless master now needed. War Bonnet was frightened and prancing nervously, wondering where Colt had gone. Contrary to the portrayal in many of the western dime novels, most great horses were not really that smart. In fact, most cowboys didn't want a horse that was too smart, because they were usually troublemakers. The best thing about War Bonnet was not his brain, but his heart. The paint gelding had no quit to him, and he would sense when he and Colt were going into battle, and relished it. Like a mighty dog, he was totally loyal and dedicated to his master. That was what made War Bonnet a great horse.

On the other side of the tall cliffs, War Bonnet pranced in place, frightened and nervous, but he would never leave the spot he was left by his master. That was how he was trained.

Colt moved away from the crack immediately, not wanting to be exposed to more fire, and especially deadly ricochets. Colt could not remember the last time he had been so angry with himself. He could not believe that he had stupidly left his rifle, food, and ammunition on his horse while he climbed through that narrow crack, just because he was so single-minded in his purpose to find the killer. Never again would Chris Colt do something so ignorant, but alas, the damage was done. He would have to seek out and apprehend or kill his quarry, then worry about getting out of the box canyon. In the meantime, there was food, water, and shelter available. Colt's greatest challenge would be to carefully conserve his remaining few bullets.

As he entered the trees and looked around, he felt for his big Bowie knife. He knew it might be needed before the day was over.

Colt ran deeper into the trees, then dropped to his belly and crawled quickly about twenty feet. He was immersed in the green undergrowth, and he froze in place and waited. And he waited.

After fifteen to thirty minutes, he estimated, the lawman rose slowly to his feet. Colt checked his guns and saw he had one bullet left in his left-hand gun, and that was it. He was immediately surprised by the sound of the voice behind him, just twenty feet away. He turned to see Black Fox, who had apparently also been hiding in the same bed of brush a short stone's throw away from Colt. A rifle was pointed at Chris's belly at point-blank range.

"Wamble Uncha," the angry brave challenged, "this coup is mine to count. Blood must be paid for blood. Go now, or die."

Well, this was it. Chris Colt knew that this man lost a son he loved to a cruel, sadistic killer. He knew the rage and guilt this man felt because he had felt it himself when his own family was murdered. He was a warrior and felt he had not protected his loved ones. The revenge helped to ease the guilt somewhat, but it would never really dissipate completely. Chris knew that the fire burned in this man, and that Black Fox would indeed kill him if he did not leave. But Colt could not. His job, his commitment, his oath dictated that he not leave. Right now, Chris

Colt hated his job more than anything in the world.

"Listen to me, my brother," Colt said. "Do not force me to fight you. Let me join together to get this man who killed your son."

Black Fox's eyes blazed, "You will leave now, or you will die here. You cannot block my trail."

Colt pleaded, "My brother, do not do this, please. Let us join together."

Black Fox was emotionless as he said, "The time for words is past. You will go. Now."

Colt knew he had been painted into a corner. He had an enraged father pointing a rifle at his mid-section. Colt could not try to wound the man, or he would probably take a bullet. He would have to draw and shoot to kill to preserve his own life. He stared directly into the other warrior's eyes, but remained aware of the man's index finger tight on the trigger of the carbine.

Suddenly, another movement caught Colt's eye from his right side. A figure had materialized amid the trees. Chris Colt and Black Fox both sensed the presence at the same time, and both warriors turned to look at the man who had just stepped into view. Looking into the cold black pools of Wah Pe Can's eyes, Chris Colt was reminded of another serial killer he had faced called Eagle. Both men seemed calm, almost apathetic. Their eyes belied nothing going on in their twisted minds.

Colt now had two men facing him. Both pointed rifles at him, and both wanted *him* dead. Chris knew he had one bullet in his left gun, and though he was right-handed, he could draw faster and shoot straighter with his off hand than others could with their good hand. He knew the cards were now dealt and drawn, and he had been called. It was time to show his hand.

Chris Colt, to the surprise of the two Lakotah, slowly raised his hands. Both men were puzzled, and it afforded Chris the split second he needed. He dived forward as his left hand swept down to his holster, whipping the gun out and firing before either Sioux could react. At the same time, Colt's right hand grasped his razor-sharp Bowie knife, whipping toward Black Fox at blinding speed. Both rifles barked, the bullets crossing each other just above the leaping lawman's back. Colt's bullet caught Wah Pe Can in the chest, spinning him around, sending him flying backward. Black Fox tried to duck the knife too late, and it caught him in the right eye, burying itself in his skull. He died instantly and did not have a chance to see the killer of his son die. But Wah Pe Can was not dead yet.

Colt did not wait to see how the two men fared, because he knew the bullet he threw toward the killer was off-target. He scrambled toward Black Fox's corpse and retrieved his knife. Wah Pe Can was rising now, blood bubbling from his chest. He raised his rifle just as Colt flipped the knife over, catching the blade. Quickly, he threw underhanded, and the knife spun over twice before hitting the man in the left side of his chest. The blade sliced a rib and passed between another, nicking Wah Pe Can's heart as it sunk into the killer's chest.

Blood now poured from the killer's mouth and pumped out his chest, but to the amazement of Chris Colt, Wah Pe Can still raised the rifle and aimed at the lawman. Colt's heart stopped as he stared at the rifle barrel. Wah Pe Can pulled the trigger, but nothing happened. He had not recocked the carbine, so there was no round in the chamber. He then died right there on his feet, still aiming the rifle, his body collapsing into a pile.

Colt's legs gave out, as he felt the bile rise in his throat. Chris gagged and rolled over on his side, vomiting. Afterward he just lay there, shaking, looking up at the sky. After ten minutes, Colt rose to his feet, walked to the stream, and washed his face in the cold, calming water.

He dreaded what he had to do next. Tears streaming down his cheeks, the frontier legend walked over to the body of Black Fox, then dropped to one knee and raised both fists skyward screaming as loud as he could. He touched the man's body and bowed his head in silent prayer. Because of his badge and his commitment to protect and preserve the law, he had been forced to kill a man who had probably been going through the same mental anguish as Chris Colt himself had felt when his own family was cut down.

Chris knew that Black Fox had forced his hand. It was kill or be killed. What bothered him was that he himself had ridden many days and many miles, hunting down every member of the renegade Crow war party who had raped and murdered his first wife, Chantapeta, and his daughter Winona. Colt had exacted revenge on each of those renegades and he was cold and ruthless about it. This father had been doing the same thing, but could not see through his rage to let Colt help him avenge his son's death.

After he composed himself, Colt used several sticks and the butt of Wah Pe Can's rifle to dig a grave for the body of the fallen warrior. He placed Black Fox in the bottom of the grave, and then removed his badge. Reading the inscription, "Deputy U. S. Marshal," Colt tossed it into the grave. Chris had made up his mind. He just could no longer wear a badge, not after this shooting.

He spoke quietly, "I am so very sorry, my brother. Why did you make me kill you? You were a grieving father, just like me." He paused before going on. "Why couldn't you let the law help avenge your son's death? I can't fully believe in my job anymore if pursuing justice gets innocent men killed. It's over. I swear I will never, ever wear a badge again."

Chris made camp and went to sleep. He awoke just before dawn—that time of the early morning before the glow of the rising sun begins on the eastern horizon. Starting a fire to ward off the chill, he looked around and found some wild turnips and onions, pulling them from the ground. As it started to get light, he found a stand of trees and stripped several large round chunks of birch bark. Returning to the fire, he used the bark to form a vessel and filled the bark bowl with water and set it on the fire, knowing the outside of the bark would not burn below the line of the water inside. He then dropped the onions and turnips in. Colt smiled as he found some sassafras, knowing he would soon be enjoying some warm stew.

He then took some sticks from low branches and broke them off until he had quite a few with sharp ends. He stuck these into the bottom of the shallow creek in the shape of an inverted arrowhead, then used large rocks to make a wall behind it and had a nice little fish trap, hoping he would have some nice brook trout by lunchtime.

After eating, Colt started walking around the perimeter of the box canyon to try to find an escape route. He finally found a ledge well over fifty feet up where the trees rose straight up to the sheer cliff. Maybe, he thought, if he could get up there, he could find a way up and over. He worried about War Bonnet, knowing the mighty stallion was highly disciplined and might well remain ground-reined where he was, not leaving for graze or water before it was too late.

The horse was now, in fact, prancing around the walled enclosure, looking for a way to get to Colt. He saw the rock fall during the earthquake and knew his master was trapped within. War Bonnet was almost panicked, but he was used to being left sometimes for hours, and he knew his master would always return to pat him gently, scratch his ears, and eventually return him to pasture to eat succulent alfalfa-grass hay, along with oats, corn, and molasses mixed in his warm comfortable stall.

War Bonnet found a small game trail on the southern side of the outside of the rock wall and tried to ease his way up. This was unnatural, as a horse—especially a panicked one—will always take the easiest route, most normally downhill. His instinct, however, told him to try to make it up the deer trail. War Bonnet's legs shook as rocks he stepped on gave way and tumbled down the mountainside. It was not comfortable for him to walk on unsure footing, but with the memory of his master's careful reining and light leg touches, he knew he could walk over anything without fear.

Colt found a very tall tree which had died several years before. It was as thick as a one-horse buggy. He would have to chop it down somehow. If he could fell the tree against the cliff, it would serve him well as a giant ladder to ascend and escape the confines of the box canyon. Colt started chopping with his Bowie, but the dead tree was too large. Colt remembered something he had once heard about a trick used by woodland Indians back East.

Chris fashioned some more water vessels from birch bark and returned to the tree, carrying the bowls, now filled with water. He then took some dried pine cones and twigs and started a fire in the area of the trunk that he had chopped with his Bowie knife. As the fire started burning into the slot he had hacked, he kept pouring water above and around the cut to keep the whole tree from going up in flames. He kept this up for several hours, and was pleasantly surprised as he dug away at the ashes with his knife.

Colt continued the process until, after two more hours, the big tree fell toward the cliff. It toppled against the cliff with a resounding crash and Chris grinned with newfound hope.

He immediately started climbing the large tree, which, leaning against the high cliff wall, provided a handy ramp to the top. Colt had to move slowly and carefully near the top, as dead branches cracked underfoot and in his hands. Chris finally made it to the ledge and carefully pulled himself up. He lay on his back, panting for a quarter of an hour.

Suddenly, a shadow blocked out the sun, and he heard a familiar whinny bringing a big smile to his face.

"How did you ever get up here, boy?"

The gentleness and attitude of Colt's voice immediately calmed the panicked horse. He pawed at the rock and tossed his black-and-white mane from side to side.

"Am I ever glad to see you, boy," Colt said.

The horse nickered, and Chris noticed a small amount of blood on the horse's two forelegs where he had banged them against sharp rocks as his feet slipped on the way up. He petted the paint, then grabbed the reins and slowly led him down the trail. At the bottom, Colt mounted up and followed War Bonnet's backtrail to a nearby stream.

Next, he unsaddled the big paint and let him roll in the grass by the stream. Fortunately, there were no saddle sores on his back or side. Nevertheless, Colt would make camp right by the stream and let the horse rest without saddle or bridle.

Colt went to bed, relieved about his escape, but still sad about killing Black Fox. He remembered vividly all the emotions that ran through him while he was trying to catch the murderers of his wife, and the killers of his first family. In both cases, Chris felt very ashamed as he had not been there to protect his loved ones. He had this feeling that he could always protect those he loved, yet he had not done it. Finding, fighting, and vanquishing the killers provided some closure for him. Although he still carried the burden of guilt, it at least brought some relief, as he felt as if he had done something about it anyway. He also felt better because killing the murderers would prevent them from doing this to any other families. What Chris had done was exactly what Black Fox had tried to do, but now his wife had to mourn both a son and a husband. Colt fell asleep, thoughts churning through his mind.

In the morning, he saddled up and headed for Black Fox's village to deliver the sad news. From there, he would head south to Cheyenne and catch a train down to Pueblo, then ride out south of Hardscrabble to Westcliffe and on toward his ranch.

CHAPTER 3

Home

Several days later, stopping in Denver, Colt went to the federal judge and officially turned in his resignation. The judge, the judge's clerk, and even a local policeman all tried to talk him out of it, but Colt's mind was set from the moment he buried his badge with Black Fox.

By the time Chris Colt reached Pueblo, the word that he had resigned was out in a number of newspapers, and even more quickly in all the bars and saloons in Colorado. When he got off the train in Pueblo, he received a telegram that his brother Joshua was in Canon City buying some land. Colt loaded War Bonnet on a train headed west and climbed aboard for the short ride to Canon City.

Arriving there, Colt met his brother and Chris's good friend, the attorney Brandon Rudd, all eating lunch at a small café near the river.

Brandon asked the question first. "Chris, is it really true what we read?"

"Yes," Colt replied.

"But why?" Brandon asked.

Joshua answered, "There is some good reason, and he probably doesn't want to talk abut it. He'll tell us in his own time."

Chris gave his older brother a smile.

"Of course," Brandon said quietly.

After hearing news that everyone at the ranch was doing fine, especially his children, Chris stood up, not bothering to finish his food.

Explaining, he said, "Joshua, I'm going to head home by way of Oak Creek Grade. I'll stop in Westcliffe, and explain my resignation to the sheriff."

He stood to shake hands with Brandon and Joshua.

"Take your time. We'll see you when you get there," Joshua said.

Colt had no idea that a pair of eyes were staring at his back from behind a newspaper, two ice-cold, venomous eyes. Being careful not to be noticed by the handsome attorney or the black rancher, the man followed Chris from the café. He had overheard Colt's declaration about his planned route home, so all he needed to do was set up an ambush along Oak Creek Grade, not too far from Canon City. He could get away and mix his tracks with all those around town. Colt, he decided, would finally pay for the pain he had caused him so long ago.

Colt started south and crossed the Arkansas River, preferring to ford the fast current instead of riding over the Fourth Street Bridge. He wanted to be alone as he got closer to home, and he knew his brother would explain it all to Brandon Rudd. Joshua and Chris were much alike in many ways, and knew each other's moods. Joshua, without the words being spoken between them, would understand all the mental and emotional turmoil of his younger brother. Joshua would know simply because he would assume such for Chris to give up law enforcement just like that.

Colt came up out of the river and started gradually heading uphill. The green tall oaks and cottonwoods and the green grasses by the river soon gave way to sparser clumps of bunch grass, pinions, and cedars.

Colt started up in the shadows of the range of foothills off to his right, overshadowed by Tanner Peak. Chris headed up Oak Creek Grade, a stage road that would take him right to the edge of Silver Cliff. It was a beautiful scenic ride that would take him home the long way, but give him some time to think about his future. The Indian Wars were over, as was his career, now. Colt felt somewhat lost. He had mixed emotions. He knew he would long for the chase, and would miss the exhilaration of battle, but it all had to end.

Colt squeezed his calves against the ribs of the big horse and the paint gladly quickened to a mile-eating trot, tired of all the time and confinement in the stuffy railroad car. They quickly put the homes and outer ranches of Canon City behind them as they headed south up Oak Creek Grade. The stage road passed between two hogback ridges and made a hairpin turn to the right, and it was there that Colt spotted the rider who had been paralleling him along the ridge to his right. A few miles outside town, the road veered sharply to the left, and Colt avoided the hairpin, instead traveling straight uphill. Someone was watching him, maybe planning to bushwhack him, and he meant to find out who it was.

He turned off the grade and dismounted, leaving War Bonnet hidden in some trees, then quickly scrambled up the hogback. A cloud of dust followed him out of Canon City, so Colt waited to see who was causing it.

It wasn't long before the dust cloud came around the bend a hundred yards away. Galloping at him was a small posse, and Colt could see badges glinting on the chests of several in the lead. Chris was surprised to see one of them was his brother. The group of men slid to a stop in front of Colt, who was now sitting on a boulder, smoking a cigarette.

Joshua explained, "They came to the café right after you left. Seems some fella was hiding there that left a bullet in somebody's gizzard down by the hot springs."

"A bullet?" Chris said.

Joshua explained, "Well, some puncher came up and just asked him why the man was so fidgety, and he just got mad, drew his gun, and gutshot the man. Anyway, he was seen headed this way, so I came to warn you."

Chris pointed behind him and took a puff, saying, "He's up there in the trees."

The deputy started to take off, saying, "Let's go get him."

"Hold on, Deputy," Colt said. "Could I offer a suggestion?"

"Yes, sir, Marshal Colt," the young deputy said.

Chris stopped him, saying, "I'm not a marshal anymore. Just a regular citizen."

Nonplussed, the deputy said, "Yes, sir, what should we do?"

Chris said, "The man has been shadowing me, and he might think I'm on his trail. If you boys go charging up the hill, he's going to go up over the ridge and head back into the Chandler Creek gulches, and you'll never find him. If you go up the Grade and wait, I'll head up that way, and flush him out toward you. The terrain will funnel him right toward you, and you can set up an ambush near that squatter's cabin up the Grade a couple miles."

"Yes sir, Marshal. I mean, Mr. Colt. That makes sense. We'll head there and wait for you," the deputy replied.

Joshua came to his brother and said, "I'll ride with you a ways."

"Josh, I want some time alone," Chris said steadily.

Joshua responded, "I know, but it's silly to ride into an ambush. I'll ride with you till we see what this hombre's gonna do." Joshua was on a sure-footed buckskin about seven or eight years old. His horse could stop on a dime and give you nine cents change.

They headed uphill toward old Indian encampments that were located at a number of natural springs overlooking Canon City several miles to the north.

The outlaw had seen the posse headed up Oak Creek Grade, but hadn't seen Chris Colt since he disappeared behind the hogback. Maybe, he thought, Colt was stopping for lunch, because he had not eaten any of his food back at the café. If he went south along the face of the foothills, he would be able to see what was going on down below on Oak Creek Grade, and he could cover one of the main springs where Colt might decide to water his horse. The killer hid his own horse among the trees along the cliff face and returned to several tall oak trees overlooking the spring, which trickled out of the side of the mountain. The assassin sat down behind a large tree and pulled branches around him for more cover.

Chris's eyes searched the surrounding terrain as he rode along, quietly telling his brother about the earthquake, and how he had killed the two Sioux. He felt trickles of sweat start down his side from both underarms, the hot sun now high in the sky. They had ridden their horses down the ridgeline that ran opposite to the one where the bushwhacker waited.

Colt led the way down a switchback trail, zig-zagging down the steep side of the long ridge that went off to the south, his leather chaps scraping along a large cactus at the bottom. He hollered back a warning, noticing Joshua hadn't started down the hill, yet. He waited at the bottom of the draw below his brother until Joshua had built a cigarette and joined him. Red-throated hummingbirds playfully dive-bombed them.

Colt turned War Bonnet, squeezing his ribs lightly with his calves. The big paint started walking through the small valley several hundred feet down below. They turned at the bottom of the valley, following a small trickle of water uphill to the spring. The little creek wound its way through the scattered pinions and cedars and rocks, and so did Colt and Joshua, walking the horses through wet grass along the edges of the waterflow.

War Bonnet suddenly became prancy, anticipating something. Colt's eyes strained hard into the scrub oak thicket next to them, but he saw nothing. War Bonnet was starting to act up even more now, even snorting several times. He was a very spirited horse, so Chris wasn't surprised at his behavior, but it certainly seemed as if something was making him very nervous. The ex-chief of scouts had seen a mountain lion bounding across the face of the mountain once, and he had also seen bears when he had camped there before with the Ute and Cheyenne. He thought maybe one of them was near and the animal's scent was spooking his horse.

The saddle leather creaked as War Bonnet danced nervously and strained at the bit. Joshua rode behind Chris as the narrow passageway along the creek between two brush thickets had funneled together.

"Easy, partner," Colt whispered, patting his horse's neck to reassure him. "Relax, War Bonnet. There's no goblins out there ready to eat horses, just maybe a bushwhacker. Do you smell him, boy?"

The bushwhacker, in a checkered shirt and old Confederate army trousers, indeed was close, now kneeling behind the tree to Colt's left, only about fifty feet above him. Little did Colt know that the man was now closing one eye while setting his sights right on the center of the lawman's face, pulling slowly back on the trigger. Simply put, God blessed the tall cowboy again. The little round pin in the front sight of the rifle was lined up with the "v" of the rear sight. The sniper started to squeeze off the shot, and the firing pin hit the primer of the forty-four caliber bullet. Chris Colt heard a very loud "cracking" sound as the bullet broke the sound barrier, passing within an inch of his left ear, followed by an almost simultaneous "whump" from the muzzle blast. A second wild shot let him hear the muzzle blast again, and he immediately cataloged the gun as a .44 caliber. The bullet had whizzed past him and flew immediately to the right of Joshua, just missing him. He grabbed the saddle horn as the old buckskin decided to act green, pitching sideways, wild-eyed, trying to bolt. In a way, the buckskin horse was kind of like Joshua; it just never got used to the idea of being shot at.

The sniper hurried off, making his way across the face of the mountain on a six-inch-wide deer trail that wound through the trees.

Colt turned his head to check on Joshua, who now had his Peacemaker out and had the horse calmed down.

"Are you hurt?" Chris yelled.

Eyes wide, Joshua called back, "Nope, missed me!"

Turning uphill, Colt put the spurs to his horse, pulling one .45 from its holster. War Bonnet charged up the mountainside after the shooter, but suddenly slammed the brakes on as he spotted the sniper preparing to fire another shot. The gun blasted and the bullet whined in front of man and horse, narrowly missing, thanks to the big pinto having stopped so quickly.

Colt and War Bonnet smelled the gun smoke drifting downhill on the breeze. The big horse had braced himself with his forelegs, sticking his neck straight forward, ears pointed straight ahead, both nostrils flaring in and out. His eyes showed panic, and Colt could hear him snorting very loudly in abject fear.

Chris slapped his neck and spurred him, yelling, "Good boy, War Bonnet. Go!"

The horse needed only that reassurance and reared up facing uphill on the steep slope, before taking off after the sniper.

Colt had no idea who had done the shooting, but he was furious and felt violated. It was just preposterous that someone would be after him after he had just turned in his badge.

Spurring War Bonnet up the mountain, Colt yelled, "Come on, damn you! Shoot me, coward! I'll gut you and leave you for the buzzards!"

Colt knew the first principle in an ambush was gaining immediate fire superiority. The sniper with his rifle had the advantage, so Colt felt that yelling and charging the man was one way to attempt getting the upper hand. Cursing and screaming while challenging the sniper to shoot him could possibly unnerve the man, and it apparently had as the sniper simply took off running, not even trying to fire at the pursuing Chris Colt.

When Chris reached the deer trail above the spring, he quickly found the shooter's hiding place, and his tracks taking off on the trail. This guy might have been stupid to fire at Chris Colt, but he knew what he was doing.

Chris looked back at Joshua, coming fast behind him, and yelled, "Quick, Josh, go warn the posse!" Joshua started to protest, but Colt cut him off. "I'm okay. Go ahead!"

Joshua knew that this was Chris Colt's area of expertise, and he didn't argue anymore, knowing Chris would not argue with him if they were in the midst of a cattle stampede.

Chris Colt ran War Bonnet back along the cliff face in the direction of a nearby ridge running to the northeast. Here the sniper could hide anywhere and pick him out of the saddle. Colt had no idea who the shooter could be, and why he was after him, but the man was going to die just the same.

The trees were so thick and branches so low on the deer trail, that Colt had to dismount and lead War Bonnet part of the way. The trail led through a cedar thicket, and he actually had to use his kerchief to tie the stirrups up over the seat in the saddle to keep them from catching on branches. The six-inch-wide trail, with sheer drops of fifty to several hundred feet straight down at some places, was not a problem for the brave paint, but the few areas of thick trees slowed War Bonnet down considerably.

As they came out of the trees again, Colt swung up in the saddle and continued heading along the trail, War Bonnet's hooves sending numerous rocks and pebbles tumbling down the cliff face to their left. He could look out over the valley to his left and see all the houses and buildings in Canon City, the land growing greener and greener as it gently sloped toward the banks of the fast-flowing Arkansas River.

Seeing some good tracks left behind by the sniper on the saddle of the ridge, Chris again dismounted and checked the tracks closely. The man was wearing small hobnailed boots. He found where the man had run down the steep side of the ridge, jumping sideways and making deep holes in the soft shale. He had also crossed an area of very wet gray clay below the natural springs.

Just beyond the clay, he saw tracks in the muddy edges of the gulch below the spring where the sniper had stopped and knelt down behind a sapling. The bushwhacker knew he was being followed and was obviously going to ambush Colt on his backtrail. Chris led War Bonnet to the spot and tied the horse's reins up behind the saddle horn.

The former chief of scouts had a plan to ambush the ambusher, and as usual, it started with common sense. Colt knew that people and animals have a tendency to look around them for danger, but seldom look up. For this reason, Colt decided to climb up the cliff, then cut diagonally across it, staying well above the bushwhacker and overtaking the man's position.

Colt's adrenaline was pumping and his mind was clear, as it always was in a combat situation. The fear, the shaky knees, stomach cramps, and weakness in the muscles would come later, after he was in a safe place and could let down. For now, Christopher Colt was what he was trained to be—a killing machine.

Scrambling as quick and as quietly as he could, Colt raced across the cliff face, his sides heaving from exertion. He was still young, but now bruises and sore muscles always seemed to last longer. His reflexes weren't quite as fast, but he had knowledge and experience that few warriors would ever possess, and that made all the difference in the world.

After a half hour, Colt finally spotted movement down below. The sniper, he saw, was small and had black hair peeking out from underneath a floppy hat with small cedar and pinion branches tied around the brim. He wore dirty clothes that were also covered with branches. Very clever, Colt thought. He hadn't seen that done before, although he had seen Indians use animal hides for camouflage. The rifle in his hand was a Winchester carbine like Colt's own.

The tall scout worked his way down the ridge beyond the ambusher and stopped when he reached the deer and elk trail where the sniper had hidden.

Colt had trained War Bonnet to come when Colt whistled like a red-tailed hawk. It was a useful trick when Colt didn't want to chance scaring game or men. As Colt whistled, the horse started forward on the trail. Colt knew War Bonnet would walk right toward the sniper, as a horse will naturally follow the path of least resistance.

In the meantime, Chris crept forward patiently. He would make the last few steps as the bushwhacker spotted the approaching horse.

It didn't take long. After five minutes, Colt had the sniper in sight. Yet something really bothered him in the way the little sniper was crouched down behind a pinion sapling. He was squatting with his heels and soles flat on the ground in the bottom of a very deep knee bend. This was exactly how Little Legs Ben Stevenson, a man Chris had killed in a stand-up gunfight when the man resisted arrest, used to squat.

The bushwhacker sensed something coming, and his rifle came up to his shoulder, aiming along his backtrail. Within seconds, he could hear approaching hoofbeats. Colt inched forward, the Bowie knife blade held firmly in his right hand, ready for a quick overhand throw. The Peacemaker was in his left hand for a backup, but he didn't want to give away his position in case there were any other bushwhackers around.

War Bonnet came into view, and the sniper tensed his body, aiming the rifle. When he realized that Colt was not in the saddle, his body language showed he was going to spin around, but Colt's hand was too fast. His right arm whipped forward, the blade slipping smoothly through his thumb and fingers. The blade spun over twice in the air and buried itself halfway to the hilt in the man's back, just above his right kidney next to his spine.

Colt closed on the shooter before the man could drop, his right arm wrapping around the man's throat and grabbing his own left bicep. Colt now had the sniper in a deadly choke, with the scout's right arm tight across the carotid artery, the crook of his elbow crushing down on the man's windpipe. By simply squeezing, Chris could cut off the blood to the man's brain and his breathing, but instead he showed some mercy.

"Who are you, damn you, and why'd you try to dry-gulch me?" Colt demanded.

Struggling to speak, the man said, "You kilt mah twin, and ah'ma gonna kill ya anyhow."

The man suddenly cross-drew a Navy .36 strapped on his belt and cocked the hammer back, but tightening his choke hold on the man, Chris kicked his legs out behind him, and the pressure of his sudden body weight dropping snapped the would-be assassin's neck like a dry branch. The sniper died instantly.

Colt sat down on rubbery legs and shook for a few minutes. He soon got up and stepped on the man's back, pulling on the Bowie with both hands until it came out with a wet popping sound. Chris wiped the blade off on the green silk kerchief around the man's neck. Seeing that struck Colt funny, but he shook it off.

War Bonnet whinnied and pranced nervously at the smell of death. Chris went through the man's pockets and found an old newspaper story about Colt killing Little Legs in the gun-fight. There was also an obituary.

In a shirt pocket, he found a lone match and an unsigned note stating: "If you want to pay back the man who murdered your brother, just come to Westcliffe and wear a green scarf. You will be contacted."

It was simply signed: "A friend who wants justice, too."

Colt then looked skyward and said a silent prayer of thanks. He petted War Bonnet for a couple of minutes while he thought and lit up a cigarito with a match.

Chris decided the body wouldn't keep where it was and would soon be found by coyotes and buzzards, so he located the sniper's tethered horse nearby and brought it to the body. He wrapped the sniper up in the man's bedroll and tied him across the saddle.

Going up and down several ridges, leading the horse, Colt finally came out on Oak Creek Grade at the hairpin. Chris slowed the horse to a walk and finally stopped, letting War Bonnet take a well-deserved rest. Colt needed one, too. The shakes started again.

Oak Creek Grade was a scenic road that

began in Canon City and climbed in elevation, winding its way through scenic forestland before eventually ending in the Wet Mountain Valley at the adjoining towns of Silver Cliff and Westcliffe. A silver and gold mining area with some of the most beautiful mountain vistas anywhere, at an elevation of just under eight thousand feet, the towns lay nestled in the high valley at the foot of the gorgeous Sangre de Cristo Mountain Range.

Chris decided to tie the horse with the body in some trees by the hairpin and let the posse pick it up on the way back to town. He tied a piece of leather to a branch by the stage road to mark where to find the body and headed toward the old empty homesteader cabin up the Grade.

Suddenly, Colt heard a gunshot and spurred War Bonnet at a full gallop up over a hill and cross-country toward the cabin. As he rounded some trees and came into a deserted two-rut ranch road, Colt saw before him a host of posse members. There was a young man on a horse under a tree, a noose around his neck, his hands tied behind his back. Joshua was holding a Peacemaker on the posse, and they all looked like they were wondering if they should take a chance against the steely-eyed rancher. Colt rode up fast, and War Bonnet set his hindlegs down, making a long sliding stop in a cloud of dust between the posse members. One of them coughed from the rising dust.

"Well, boys," Colt said, "looks like my brother is trying to keep you from doing something you'll always regret."

The deputy piped up, saying, "Well, Mr. Colt, the court has been kind of slow around here, and we want men to know you don't gut-shoot someone in Canon City and steal his horse."

One of the other men piped up, "Yep, an' I seen this yahoo tryin' ta brace you up ta Westcliffe, Colt. 'Member when ya hit 'im with all them stones? I'll tell ya, ef'n the Vigilance Committee were here, we wouldn't even be jawjackin.' He'd be dancin' at the end of that there rope."

Chris Colt looked at the young man wearing the noose and saw it was indeed the young man who had tried to egg him into the gunfight in Westcliffe.

Choking the words out, the man said, "Mr. Colt, I ain't ever murdered nobody. You taught me my lesson. I was headed to Denver to try to get an honest job, sir. I didn't even come from Canon City. I was *headed* there. I swear."

Colt turned toward the posse members and said, "He didn't do it."

The deputy replied, "How do you know, Mr. Colt?"

Chris nodded at the young man and said, "Doesn't have any gray clay on his shoes or pants. Look at me."

The officers all looked at his cowboy boots and denims, which was covered with the thick gray clay all the way up to his knees. His horse, still standing next to him, was also covered up to his knees.

Colt calmly added, "Besides, I already killed your backshooter and have him tied across his saddle and hidden in some trees down the Grade, so you boys can pick him up on your way home."

Some men in the posse started clearing their throats.

"Suppose somebody could take the necktie off that innocent man before his horse spooks?" Colt said.

The deputy and two others immediately ran over and took the noose off the man's neck while another untied his wrists. Joshua holstered his pistol and shook his head at Chris in exasperation at the men.

Colt said, "Now, boys, do I need to tell you the error of your ways?"

"No, sir," one of them said, shaking his head.

Another said, "Joshua, Chris, thank you for keeping me from making the biggest mistake of my life, outside of marrying my wife. She's as ugly as my mule but not as smart."

Chris and Joshua grinned.

Johnny Oxendine rode over to Colt, rubbing his neck, his eyes wide open.

He said, "Thank you again, sir, both of you. You saved my life."

Colt smiled and said, "See how a bad reputation can make things worse for you?"

Still wide-eyed, the young man said, "Sir, you already set me on the straight and narrow. I never wanted to leave a state so much in my whole life. I want Colorado behind me as quick as I can get out of here. I swear, I'll never come back for the rest a my life, I can tell you that. So long."

He put the spurs to his horse and headed toward Canon City, leaving Chris and Joshua grinning after him.

"I believe you led that young man to the Way, the Truth, and the Light, brother," Joshua mused.

"I hope, but a month from now will tell what

he's really going to do. Easy to be scared of fire while your finger's still burnt," Chris replied.

Chris pointed out to the posse where the sniper's body was, and the two brothers started up Oak Creek Grade.

CHAPTER 4
Questions

Colt and Joshua went north from Reed Gulch Road, stopping to help an old bow-legged rancher they had seen only once before, whose horse had tossed a shoe. He lived up to the north in Nesterville.

Cotton Smith was bent over trying to pry the other hind shoe off with a large knife when Joshua dismounted, taking a hoof pick from his saddlebags to do the job. The leathery-skinned oldster nodded, grinned, and sat down on a log, pulling "the fixings" from his pocket.

Cotton pointed at the pinto with his tobacco pouch, saying, "I've seen that paint, son. That horse was owned by Ole Crazy Horse hisself, wasn't it?"

It was the second time that Chris had ever seen the old man, but it was obvious he was the kind of "real cowboy" the ex-lawman had moved west to meet and become, minus the slow drawl and worn-out ranch clothes.

Colt replied, "Yes, sir, he was. Crazy Horse gave him to me a few years before his death. I don't think that Crazy Horse had the heart to watch him move onto a reservation, retire, and starve to death trying to graze on sand."

Cotton chuckled and built a smoke. Lighting it, he looked at the mountains to the west.

After a few more thoughtful puffs, the leathery-skinned old-timer said, 'I'll tell you what, son. That ole horse has crunched a good bit of gravel under them hooves up in them mountains yonder. You make sure he always gets fed and watered proper."

Chris smiled and nodded.

"Lessee, how old is yer hand Tex Westchester now?" Cotton said.

Joshua stood up, easing a cramp from his lower back, saying, "He's in his late seventies or early eighties, sir. Still sits a horse and pushes cows around everyday."

Cotton said, "Well, he's an old man like me so now, I'll guaran-damn-tee he has to stand on a rock to git into the saddle of a mornin'. Did you know he was a colonel in the war? Fought at Gettysburg, I do believe. You ever been in the war, son?" Then answering his own question, he went on, "Naw, yer too young."

Colt interjected, "Yes, sir, I was. Lied about my age. I served with the 171st Infantry Regiment of the Ohio National Guard."

Joshua finished shoeing the horse, then remounted the buckskin as Cotton said, "Obliged, sonny." Addressing Chris again, he went on, "Thet's why ya do what ya do. Can't hep yerself, son. Took way too many chances in the war and warn't kilt, and ya was real good at what ya done. Ya gits ta miss it all the time. Fella sorta gits used ta gettin' shot at and such. Even if ya don't like it, or say ya don't. Makes ya feel alive. Ya need thet ever oncet in a while. Kinda' clears out the cobwebs. Gotta git. See ya, boys."

Watching the back of the old-timer continue on toward Westcliffe, the old man's conversation stuck with Chris. His simple drawled but clear-cut words knifed deep into Chris Colt like one of his own Bowies. Colt knew that the man was right.

Snapping Chris from his thoughts, Joshua said, "So are you going to ranch with me now, or what?"

Colt answered, "I really don't know, Josh. I don't want to get in your way, and you certainly seem to be making us both plenty of money running the ranch by yourself."

"That don't matter. There's plenty of work for both of us to do," Joshua said.

Chris grinned and replied, "Thanks, big brother, but I don't want to step on your toes."

Joshua protested, "You won't be!"

"It's okay, really. I'm just not a cowpuncher. I'll find something to do. After I see Charley and the kids, I'll figure it out," Chris said.

Joshua grinned in a knowing way. "Heading up to the high-lonesome to sort things out, huh?"

When Joshua and Chris rode down the two-mile-long path leading to the ranch house, Chris suddenly whispered, "Don't look at the bushes on our right. And don't draw if you see anything out of the corner of your eye."

Joshua looked straight ahead, whispering back, "Okay."

He wondered what his brother was talking about, but moments later, he saw two little shadows sneaking out of the bushes behind them as they passed by. It was Joseph and Brenna.

To their rear, Joseph said, "You're getting careless, Colt."

Chris, feigning surprise, spun around drawing

his pistol, careful not to aim it toward his children. He grabbed toward his heart and breathed heavily as if he were frightened out of his wits.

Laughing, he then said, "Well, you two sure put the sneak on us. How about giving your pa a hug?"

Colt slid out of the saddle, holding his arms out as his two offspring ran up to him. Chris squeezed his little boy and girl tight, kissing Brenna on the forehead.

"Welcome home, Pa," Joseph said, holding out his hand to his father.

Colt's hand enveloped his little boy's, and he shook it firmly, saying, "Hello, son. Make sure you grip a little tighter. Always look a man in the eye and give him a good handshake. Women, too. Folks'll respect you more."

"Yes, sir," Joseph said squeezing a little tighter.

Later, sitting on the back veranda, drinking lemonade, Joseph asked his father, "Pa, why did you quit your job?"

Chris looked up at the mountains, seeing wisps of snow blowing off the white-capped Wulsten Baldy Peak. "I had to kill a man that shouldn't have been killed, son."

Joseph said, "But you wouldn't have kilt him if he didn't make you."

Chris gently corrected his son, "Killed, not kilt."

"Yes, sir," Joseph said, "but you still wouldn't have done it unless you had to, right?"

Colt said, "Son, you know me all too well."

Brenna, sitting on her father's lap, gave Chris a big hug. He grinned and touched her on the end of her nose.

When they finished talking, Colt got up and decided to walk to the big barn to check on War Bonnet. On the way, he saw old Tex Westchester walking toward him, along with another oldster, a Crow, in fact. Chris recognized him immediately, his old friend Long-Legged Bear.

"Howdy, boss," Tex said.

Colt shook and said, "Howdy, Colonel."

Tex bristled, then went on, "Call me Tex, please."

Colt said, "Sure, but I was saying it with respect, not teasing."

Tex said, "I know. That was then, this is now."

Looking at the old Crow, Colt smiled in wonder. "Why are you all the way down here, old man?"

The Crow replied, "Why do you think I am here Mighty Colt?"

Chris shook his head, saying, "Here we go again. I really don't know."

The old warrior held his hand out and Colt finally offered him a cigar and a light, still shaking his head in wonder.

Finally, the old man said, "You do not know, really?"

Colt answered quickly, "Maybe you were tired of the town up there and wanted to live at our big ranch."

The old man said, "Maybe."

Colt said, "Well, why are you here?"

"Why do you think?"

Chris shook his head again and laughed. "I think you are here because you were tired of the white man's town. You know that I treat your people the same as my people. You knew we had a big beautiful ranch here, lots of game for hunting, lots of fish, mild winters, and you knew you would be welcome here."

The old man shook his head as if Colt were the dumbest creature on the planet, saying, "Why does Colt ask foolish things?"

He turned, walking away, with Colt saying after his back, "Well, was that the answer?"

Mumbling to himself, then over his shoulder to Colt, the Crow elder said, "Colt always ask questions when Colt knows answers. I am glad words not food. We all die from hunger. You steal them all."

Tex and the children laughed heartily at Colt, who was confused and frustrated, but started laughing at himself, too.

Colt then yelled at the old man, "Why are you leaving?"

The old man turned and walked back with all eyes upon him, as he limped back to the group. It seemed like all were waiting on a profound answer. Walking up to Colt, he reached inside the hidden breast pocket inside Colt's war shirt and pulled out another cigar, placing it neatly into his own breast pocket.

Long, flowing white hair blowing in the wind, he simply said, "Why did I leave?"

Colt, a little frustrated, said, "Probably just to make me shout after you and ask another question. Just to make me look stupid, I suppose."

The old man touched his finger to his nose and turned, saying, "He grows wiser already."

Chris's face grew beet red as Tex slapped his leg and guffawed, and was joined by the children and Colt's younger sister who had just walked up to join the conversation. Chris started to storm off, totally embarrassed, but then proceeded to laugh at himself along with all the others.

As the old Crow walked into the large barn, Colt recalled their first meeting not long before, when he and Man Killer were pursuing Aramus Randall and Buck Fuller, two of the men who'd killed Shirley Colt. Long-Legged Bear would certainly be interesting to have around, Colt thought, if the old man didn't end up driving him crazy.

The silver-haired warrior was busy shoveling out a stall when Chris followed asking, "Do you have a place to sleep here, Long-Legged Bear?"

The warrior said, "I have been here as many suns as the fingers on my hands two times. I have not slept. I have not laid down."

Colt was shocked.

He said, "What? Nobody gave you a bed or place in the bunkhouse?"

The old man said, "Yes, Tex did. He is my friend."

Colt said, "But you said you haven't laid down."

The old man started laughing to himself as he wheeled a barrow load of manure out of the barn. He returned seconds later, still chuckling.

"Why are you laughing?"

The Crow said, "Why do you think?"

Colt said, "Oh no, not again." He started currying the big paint and said, "You were funning me, because I should have known someone gave you a place to sleep and meals."

The old man laughed again, whispering loudly, "He grows wiser still."

Chris Colt turned, laughing, and finished brushing out his horse.

The next morning found Chris Colt and Joseph halfway up the side of the big range heading toward one of their favorite fishing spots, Rainbow Lake. Colt needed to get away from the madding crowds, the civilization, the stress of everyday living, in order to sort out his future. He was a man used to work. He needed a purpose to feel right.

In years past, when Chris Colt headed up into the high-lonesome to deal with a problem, he always went alone. But his son was getting older, and Colt had experience and knowledge he needed to pass on, and he truly enjoyed his son's company. The lad was wise and mature beyond his few years.

By noon, the Colts had a roaring fire going and Chris was cleaning some cut-throat trout to toss in the frying pan. They had brought "bear tracks," some delicious doughnut-like pastries that had been made by Charley Colt. Chris also brought biscuits, vegetables, and even an extra canteen filled with milk for Joseph. As soon as they got to the high country lake, Chris placed the canteen in the water, chilling the milk so it became ice-cold and delicious.

After lunch, Chris drank coffee and Joseph drank milk while they stuffed themselves on bear tracks. The pastries were so good, they didn't even talk while they ate.

Afterward, Chris enjoyed a cigarette while they spoke.

"What kind of work are you going to do now, huh, Pa?" Joseph said.

Chris smiled. "Don't know, son. You know, a man needs to work to feel good about himself, and he needs to feel like his work means something."

Joseph thought for a minute before saying, "Everybody?"

Chris replied, "Yep. If a man is a blacksmith, he needs to understand how many horses would be lame without his shoes, how the doctor might not be able to ride his buggy to save someone's life without good steel rims on his wheels, and how the stagecoaches wouldn't be able to get through without his repairing the broken trace chains for their teams. You can figure out the importance of any job, but it is more important for a man to realize the importance of his own work."

Joseph walked over to the saddlebags and came back with a Mason jar. He had a long string tied around the rim, and Colt watched as the lad went over to the nearby meadow and started catching little bees by grabbing them in his palm as they hovered around the little clover flowers. Joseph had seven bees in the jar in a matter of minutes, and he returned to his father's side.

"C'mon, Pa," he said, "let's catch some more fish. I learned this trick from Long-Legged Bear."

Chris stood, saying, "Okay, but didn't you get stung grabbing those bees?"

"No, sir, I learned that from Long-Legged Bear, too. For some reason they just can't sting you when your hands are closed. That, or they just plain don't want to."

Colt said, "Well, see there's something new you've taught me, son. Remember that: you're never too old to learn."

They walked over to the lake, and Joseph tossed the jar full of buzzing bees in the water, tying the string off on a log.

"Long-Legged Bear says that the noise the bees make gets the fish angry, and it attracts them. When they get mad, they attack whatever you throw in the water," Joseph explained.

Within minutes, they had quite a few fish. They decided to hike south cross-county to Brush Creek Lakes and fish for some more trout there.

That night, father and son sat by a nice warm campfire, the light from the flames dancing with the shadows above them on the high pine branches, keeping time with the rhythmic crackling of sticks and branches in the fire.

Joseph hit Chris right between the eyes again with his simple profundity, saying, "Pa, what kind of things are you really good at?"

Colt said, "Well, I don't know. What do you mean?"

Joseph said, "I mean your work, Pa."

Chris cleared his throat, saying, "Well, let me see. I guess scouting and tracking. I suppose the only other thing I'm really good at is shooting."

"Do you want to shoot people?"

Chris's face turned red.

"Of course not. I hate that, Joseph. Anybody in their right mind would."

Joseph said, "I know, Pa. I'm just trying to help ya sort things out like you do with me. Can you scout much anymore?"

"Nope, not really. The Indian wars are over.

The great chiefs are all on reservations now," Colt said.

"That just leaves tracking doesn't it?" Joseph asked.

Colt gave his son a sideways glance while he lit a cigarito with a hot brand from the fire, saying, "You been taking reasoning lessons from Long-Legged Bear?"

Joseph found this very amusing and laughed for a minute or so before finally saying, "No, Pa, I learned how to think from you."

Touched, Chris looked at his son in amazement and cleared his throat, tousling Joseph's hair. "How can I make any money tracking?" Colt asked.

Joseph said, "Pa, I know I'm just a little boy, but even I know that our family is rich. Why do you need to worry about money?"

Colt chuckled again and shook his head, astounded and very proud of his offspring and his simple, straightforward intelligence.

Colt took a sip of coffee and a drag on the little cigar, then said, "Son, you're right. We do have an awful lot of money and land, and someday, you, your sister, and your cousins will own it all. But you just can't work for free because people won't value what you do, then."

Joseph thought about this and said, "What

about poor people, Pa? What if somebody don't have any money, but their kid gets lost in the mountains and needs you to find them?"

"Of course, I'll do things to help people who are poor, son, but you have to have some kind of price for your services or people never properly appreciate what you're doing."

Joseph pondered this for a few minutes while playing with the end of a burning brand from the fire.

Finally, the boy said, "Okay, then whenever you do any tracking, you tell people to pay you whatever they think the job is worth, Pa."

Colt took a long, careful drag and watched the stream of blue smoke mix with the tendrils of smoke emanating from the campfire, lazily dissipating among the myriad of branches, needles, and leaves in the green canopy over their heads.

"You know," Chris replied, "that makes perfect sense to me, partner. Well, we have a passel of fish, and it would be a shame to keep them all to ourselves, so let's get some shut-eye and take our catch down to the ranch in the morning. I'll tell them what we decided."

Joseph rolled up in his blanket, saying, "Night, Pa," feeling a warm emotion having his father say that he was included in such an important decision.

Chris, the kids, Tex, Man Killer, and Long-Legged Bear sat on the lawn overlooking Texas Creek, smelling the wonderful aromas wafting from the kitchen. The trout, smothered in butter, were frying on the pan, and Charley Colt thoroughly enjoyed herself making mouths water. She hummed to herself while sprinkling spices on the sizzling fish, turning the slices of frying potatoes in another pan.

Chris had announced his new plans to the family, and Tex wondered out loud how much money Chris Colt could really make just tracking.

Long-Legged Bear handled that question readily with one of his long series of questions. "Could Chris Colt make much more shooting with his guns?"

Tex replied, "Why, shore he would, Bear. He'd be the best around!"

"But would his heart sing, and would his children enjoy saying, 'My father kills men with his guns'?" Long-Legged Bear said.

Tex cleared his throat and said, "Naw, reckon not."

Long-Legged Bear offered, "The mighty Colt could be rancher like his brother, Joshua."

Silently listening, Man Killer chuckled at that suggestion.

Tex said, "Why, he durned shore could! He'd be good at it, too."

The old Crow replied, "How many suns would cross the sky before the two mighty Colt brothers would fight each other?"

Tex rubbed his beard stubble and gave a knowing sidelong glance, grinning at the old warrior.

"Good point, Bear," he said. "It'd happen, shore as hell. They both got oak-hard heads and would spat about somethin' round the ranch."

Long-Legged Bear then said, "Who can track like the mighty one?"

"Nobody. Nary a soul."

"If you lost a son, or horse, or prisoner, how much money would you give to get them back?"

Tex thought about this, hemming and hawing.

Long-Legged Bear, stood grinning, saying, "You have answered my question."

While the rest of the family and ranch hands were preparing for lunch, Joshua had gone off on a mission, pursuing a runaway thoroughbred stallion he had purchased not long before to add to the Coyote Run's breeding line. The horse had only been at the ranch for a week when the gate to his stall was left open. The horse wandered out until he finally made it to the long ranch road going past the house. He grazed his way northward as the terrain ran downhill toward the Arkansas River for eight or ten miles. The grasses were better along Texas Creek, so the big red stallion mainly kept to the proximity of the water.

The last four miles were much steeper, dropping down to the river, and it was there that Joshua finally tracked the valuable chestnut. He easily got a noose over its neck, and they had started back up the road toward the Coyote Run and had gone no more than a mile when Jimmy Blind Elk, camped along Texas Creek, spotted the big red horse and coveted it immediately. He looked down at the green silk scarf wound tightly around his right arm and felt the weight of the coins in his pouch given him by the white-eyes whom he did not trust. He not only would get the magnificent horse, but kill the mighty Chris Colt, as well, and receive the rest of the promised money.

Jimmy Blind Elk was a southern Ute who had been primarily raised by missionaries. Tall and lanky, he was a wild sort from the time anyone could remember. It seemed as though he was always into trouble, and many felt that trouble was just in his heart, a part of him no matter where he went.

Jimmy took two large sticks and literally pushed his campfire into the clear, cold water. Grabbing his only possession—an old beat-up feathered and brass-tacked Henry repeater—he scrambled atop the small pinion and sand-covered hillock. As Joshua rode up the road leading the horse, Jimmy took careful aim and fired. The bullet glanced across the elder Colt's forehead, and his horse reared as the big black cowboy fell backward onto the ground, unconscious.

It didn't take long for Jimmy to identify Joshua as Colt's older brother. Forgetting his disappointment about the extra bounty, he grabbed the reins of the confused chestnut stallion and led it back to his campsite. Once there, he slipped the war bridle and reins off his little roan mustang and set it loose with a slap on the rump. He climbed up on the back of the big red stud, who offered little resistance, and headed back uphill toward Westcliffe, the wind blowing in his face. He wouldn't follow the road, instead heading cross-country before he got to Westcliffe, and then crossing over Medano Pass into the San Luis Valley.

When he was parallel to Music Pass, he headed off the main trail for a hundred yards, moving back onto the trail, then off again. When he reached a small drainage, he turned south and headed toward Medano Pass, which was several miles to the south.

Jimmy then stopped after a few hundred yards and tied the horse to a bush. He ran back to the trail, stepping from grass clump to grass clump, or on rocks when they appeared. Using a large branch, he wiped out all of his tracks, a trick some outlaws used to cover their trails, but Jimmy was a Ute with a bit more knowledge. He went back again and scattered dust and sand over the area he had brushed out. He also strategically placed rocks and twigs here and there. This gave the drainage a much more natural and undisturbed appearance.

Jimmy Blind Elk carefully made his way back to the stolen horse and trotted away toward Medano Pass, knowing anyone following him would think he was crossing over Music Pass since he had headed right at it for several miles.

Jimmy planned to camp halfway across Medano Pass, and then easily find his way toward the Great Sand Dunes. He would travel due west and cross the San Juans at Wolf Creek Pass, and head straightaway toward the Ignacio area and his family on the Southern Ute Reservation.

Newly Smith was a sometimes gold miner and ofttimes brand artist who was headed toward Westcliffe on the Texas Creek Road. He had left Nesterville shortly before being asked a few too many questions by the brand inspector about his creative art work on several heifers, which looked very like some that were missing from South Park. Smith spotted Joshua Colt lying in the road and immediately thought about how much money might be in the wealthy Colt's wallet. He then remembered seeing how Chris Colt and Man Killer handled their guns, and he decided the smart thing to do would be to try to nurse the rancher and get him back to the Coyote Run. Maybe a reward would be offered.

He was correct. Three hours later, after dressing Joshua's head wound and making him some coffee and bacon, Smith took the groggy cowboy home to his family, where he was given a one-hundred-dollar reward and a big thank-you by Chris Colt himself.

Chris started packing his saddlebags and checking his weapons when Joshua said almost in a panic, "Chris, don't go! It's only a horse. We have plenty."

Chris was puzzled by Josh's reaction and could not figure out why he would not want him to go after the man who notched his skull. He asked as much.

"Look, remember when those owlhoots ambushed you in Kansas? You almost died, brother," Joshua said.

Chris replied, "Joshua, I know you have a headache, but why don't you and I wander over to the water and palaver a minute?"

The two walked over to the tree-lined creek that flowed through their property and sat down on a log bench that Colt had placed in the shade of a large cottonwood tree. Joshua held a cold wet cloth to the front of his head.

"Remember when you took all those bullets to save the woman you loved?" Chris asked.

Joshua nodded, his face red.

Colt went on, "Everybody but me thought you were going to die. Then when I spent last winter in Kansas, healing from that ambush, I almost died. Had a few other close ones, too, huh?"

Joshua nodded again.

"But you know what, big brother? We did

survive. We're Colts, and we're always going to survive."

Joshua got very sad and looked at the water, saying, "Shirley didn't."

Chris got choked up thinking about the death of his wife, but he put his arm around his older brother and said, "Yes, she didn't, and either one of us might get shot again, and take one of those bullets that sends us under. But Joshua, we can't quit doing what is right just because we're scared that it might happen."

Joshua shook his head, wiping a tear from his eye. "You know I didn't realize all the memories that bullet brought back today. One inch over and . . ."

"And you wouldn't have known any different," Chris interrupted.

Joshua laughed and said, "Guess I wouldn't have."

Chris pulled out a long weed and stuck it between his lips, handing another to his brother. They both watched a small brook trout wiggle out from behind the lee side of a rock to snatch a caddis fly off the fast-running water.

"You're right, Chris," Joshua went on. "That shot to the head scared me out of my wits."

Chris said, "I know it. I've had the same exact thing happen to me several times."

Joshua was shocked. "You have?"

"I said we were Colts. I didn't say we weren't human," Colt replied.

Joshua laughed and stood, tossing his weed in the stream.

He clapped Chris on the shoulder and said, "You better get saddled up if you're gonna track the varmint that shot me."

Man Killer emerged from the barn leading an already saddled War Bonnet, and his own horse, Hawk, the big black-and-white Appaloosa that had shared so many adventures with War Bonnet. He grinned at Colt who snatched up his saddlebags from the porch and tied them behind War Bonnet's cantle.

Chris simply said, "Going with me, huh?"

"I could always stay at my ranch and count the blades of grass in the pasture, again," Man Killer said.

Chris smiled and waved at his assembled family members as he and Man Killer rode out the driveway.

It was less than an hour before they found the spot where Joshua had fallen from the saddle. It was easy to determine the ambush spot and from where the shot was fired, and they soon found Jimmy's tracks. Backtracking him to his campsite, they found where he had turned his own horse loose. Judging by its lack of shoes, the depth of the tracks, and the fact that Jimmy dropped onto the ground when he dismounted instead of stepping out of stirrups, they knew he was riding an Indian pony bareback. They had already determined that he was an Indian earlier, because the tracks he left showed he had walked slightly pigeon-toed in soft-soled moccasins, a warrior custom. This was reinforced by the realization that he had walked toe-heel when he was approaching the hill to ambush Joshua, another Indian tactic. White men always walked heel-toe, even when they were stalking, unless they were unusual white men like Chris Colt.

The tracks headed south up the road, and were going to be easy to follow. Man Killer, the handsome young Nez Perce millionaire, simply rode along one side of the heavily traveled roadway, seeing if the stallion's tracks veered off the beaten trail. Colt rode along the other side, watching for the same thing. To make matters easier for the two, the stolen horse was wearing one cross-bar shoe on his left forehoof, as it had suffered a deep stone bruise that would take better than a month to heal. Joshua, an expert farrier, had placed the bar shoe on to protect the sensitive inside part of the hoof, called the frog.

The two former scouts cantered most of the

time. Both Hawk and War Bonnet each stood well over sixteen hands, so their long legs quickly ate up the miles. Finally, on Colt's side of the trail, the tracks finally angled off to the southwest, and the two pounded across the high valley floor after the horse thief. Darkness was closing in, and they hoped they could find where he had crossed the big range before having to make camp for the night.

Chris Colt looked up at the giant peaks looming before them, and as always could not stop being amazed at their beauty and grandeur. A chain of mountains extending all the way down through New Mexico, the peaks were all twelve to fourteen thousand-plus feet in elevation. As Chris and Man Killer approached, they looked up in awe at the crimson hue the sunset painted on the snow-capped peaks. The same phenomenon occurred in the mornings, too. This was the reason why the Spanish conquistadors christened the range Sangre de Cristo, meaning "The Blood of Christ." Colt never tired of the view, which never looked the same on any two days.

Unfortunately, the sun was now setting, and the thief's trail looked like it was heading toward Music Pass. Colt and Man Killer knew without speaking that they would have to make camp just inside the trees.

They found a spot by several evergreens with low-hanging branches, and made camp under the shelter of a thick branch. Rain or snow clouds had just started drifting over the peaks right before dark, so Man Killer climbed up one of the trees with a lasso, and roped a couple of the large branches together. Tying them with a piggin string, he formed a roof over their campsite. There were several large boulders around the campsite so the two men were protected from the elements.

They made dinner and spoke for a while before turning in. Both were enthusiastic that they had made good time, and they knew they would awaken and be in the saddle shortly after daybreak, figuring they would have the horse thief caught by noon.

Chris Colt slept fitfully, dreaming about his late wife, while Man Killer slept like a log. But both men awoke at daybreak to a total surprise. The ground all around them was powdered with several inches of snow. Early fall and late spring storms were not uncommon in the mountains of southern Colorado, and the two trackers should not have been shocked, but they were upset nonetheless. Both men knew they had to get on the trail quickly and get up and over the range, as there was probably already a foot of new snow up above, not counting the three to ten feet of snow that had been there during the winter and still had not melted away.

They could only hope that the storm had not covered the tracks of the thief.

They had no time to cook breakfast that morning, so both men grabbed beef jerky from their saddlebags, chewing on it while they rode. They quickly headed up the trail, crossing over the big range after struggling through some very large drifts. They stopped halfway down the trail on the San Luis side a bit after noon, and built a fire to get warm and fix a hot meal.

Chris and Man Killer ate in relative silence, embarrassed and concerned that they might lose the trail of the thief. It would be devastating to the egos of both men because they were so cavalier about following such an easy trail. They knew better than to not plan adequately for the eventuality of an unexpected blizzard. Chris had carefully knelt down and placed his head close to the ground, where the snow wasn't as deep. He then blew the powdery snow away from the trail and found no fresh tracks. There were none at all.

Now the men shaved a little bacon into the pan, then Chris fried some chicken he had been carrying in his saddlebags. He also cut up a potato into the hot grease, frying the slices to a golden brown. They also had some sourdough bread baked by Jennifer, Man Killer's wife, which they ate with a couple of cups of steaming hot coffee. The meal helped make them feel more enthusiastic about getting back on the robber's trail.

By mid-afternoon they were well in the midst of the massive San Luis Valley north of the Great Sand Dunes, where numerous snow-covered sandbanks several hundred feet in height stretched out for miles, sweeping up against the base of the western slope of the Sangre de Cristos. There was absolutely no sign of the horse thief, and they could only guess which way he went—north toward Poncha Springs, Salida, and Buena Vista; south toward Alamosa maybe; west toward LaGarita, Saguache, or South Fork; or he could have even backtracked from the other side and headed back toward Westcliffe. In short, the man could be anywhere.

Colt looked at Man Killer, his face crimson against the snowy white backdrop, as he said, "We've lost him. Let's go home."

Dejected and feeling like failures, the pair turned their horses, heading back toward the pass. They would try to cross over before nightfall to keep out of deeper snow and colder temperatures.

It was just after dark when they stopped to make camp halfway down the Medano Pass trail on the Wet Mountain Valley side. From their campsite in a cluster of boulders they could see the lights of Westcliffe, Silver Cliff, Hartsel, and a little beyond, Rosita. On the eastern side of the valley floor round-topped grassy knolls rose up like ghosts trying to peek up from underneath the carpet of white. The snow had stopped falling and all was an eerie white, especially in the trees where shards of moonlight knifed between evergreen needles and leaves, casting little rays and points of light on the clear, crisp snow.

After dinner, the two sat against logs, enjoying the warmth of the fire, the boulders all around them acting like giant reflectors, turning some of the fire's warmth back toward the center of the camp. They both smoked cigarettes and drank Man Killer's trail coffee. He had a formula for making trail coffee that was famous among the ranch cowboys, and Colt asked him how to make it.

Man Killer smiled. "It is easy, my brother. First, I pour in water from the melting mountain snows."

He took a long steaming sip and continued,

"Then I pour in coffee grounds. Next I add some chicory."

Man Killer stopped to drink from his tin cup and lit another smoke. "Then I search deep in the forest for still water."

Colt said, "Still water?"

Man Killer smiled. "Yes, with old dead leaves in it. I reach down in the water and dig my fingers into the mud beneath it. I scoop it out and add two handfuls."

Colt chuckled, knowing he would never get a straight answer from his friend.

"Next, I boil it until it is hot enough, and I drop in several rocks, like these in my hand, until they melt."

Colt said, "Then the coffee's ready, I suppose."

Keeping a serious face, Man Killer went on. "No, no. Then I add my secret ingredients. I cannot tell even you what they are, but I can tell you this—I cannot find the secret ingredients if my horse is not around."

Colt made a sour face, but laughed loudly.

"Then I boil it some more and pull out one of my bullets and set it on top of a cup of coffee." Man Killer pulled a bullet from his cartridge belt to dramatize his little speech and acted as if he were setting it on top of the black liquid. "When the bullet floats on top of the coffee, I know it is ready to drink."

Colt slapped his leg and laughed heartily while Man Killer struggled to maintain a straight face, a playful grin trying to break across his mouth.

Chris looked at the fire's flickering light as it played on the handsome features of the young Indian, and he thought about how many adventures the two had shared ever since Man Killer had been a young teenager. He had certainly grown into quite a man, Chris thought, without realizing what a role he himself had played as a hero, mentor, older brother, father figure, and most of all, friend.

CHAPTER 5

Tracker

In the morning they headed for home. Man Killer stopped off at his own ranch on the way to Westcliffe. Colt ate breakfast there and went on to the town to pick up the mail and learn the latest gossip.

Riding alone into Westcliffe, Chris Colt could not believe how upset he felt about blowing what would be about the easiest assignment a tracker could have—following a long-legged horse with one bar shoe, only to lose the trail in fresh snow.

Colt went by the mercantile and picked up his mail, leaving War Bonnet munching hay in the livery.

Frank Tallmaster was the merchant, and he always seemed a humorous sight to Chris Colt. The man had a very round waistline and was ashamed of it, so he always wore belts maybe fifteen inches too small. Consequently, he had layers of fat cascading down over the top of his pinched waistline, the effect not hiding his girth at all. It also forced his homespun trousers down so there was always a great deal of the cleavage of his buttocks showing, especially when he bent down to scoop out nails, nuts, or other items lined up in buckets along the wall.

Upon seeing the tracker, Frank said, "Oh, Mr. Colt, there's a message for you at the telegraph office. Ain't a telegram though, I don't think. I believe he said someone left you a message."

" 'Preciate it," Colt said. "I'll stop by later to pick up some supplies. Guess I'll catch some lunch and run some errands."

Chris walked into the tiny telegraph office. The clerk, a shock of red hair hanging out from underneath his visor, sat at his desk transcribing a message coming over the wire. As Chris walked in, he looked up, a grin spreading across his very freckled face.

"Howdy, Mr. Colt. The doc went out to patch up yer brother and he said he's gonna be fine. Yer sister come by here and said she was shoppin' in town today."

Chris said, "Okay, thanks. I want to send telegrams to lawmen all over the territory about a horse we had stolen. Let me write it down for you."

"Yes sir, Mr. Colt. Here," the man said, handing Chris a pad and pencil.

Colt wrote out the message and gave it to the clerk, thanking him and leaving the office.

Colt found Charlotte back in the same mercantile shop he had just left. They hugged.

Charley grabbed her brother's arm, a hat box in her other hand, and they walked out the door and down the board sidewalk.

"Did you and Man Killer have to kill the bushwhacker, or did you bring him in?"

Colt's face grew beet red again and his lips tightened, "Neither, Charley. We lost him."

"Oh," she said, knowing that it must be embarrassing for Chris, so she tried to figure out how to change the subject. After a pregnant pause, she said, "I don't think we should worry about that stud anyway. We have so many good stallions now."

Chris grinned down at his sister, saying, "Thanks, sis, but I need to catch the thief and return the horse. It's the principle more than anything else."

He held the door to an expensive restaurant open for her. The Powell House was the classiest hotel and restaurant in the area, and was the favorite of the whole Colt clan when they were in town.

Once they were seated, Chris went on, "Like I was saying, Charley, it's the principle. We're Colts, and we have to send a strong message to anybody that wants to attack us in the future."

They both paused to look at the menu for a few seconds, then Chris continued, "I know you were just trying to protect my ego, sis, but it's okay. A lot of tracking is getting on a false trail or making mistakes and starting over. We'll get the thief. I sent telegrams all over the territory to lawmen to watch for him and the horse. He's a Ute, and the horse is unmistakable, as the bar horseshoe he is wearing will make his tracks easy to pick up on."

Charlotte almost grinned, and Chris suddenly chuckled, saying, "Yeah, I know. Unless you're a mighty tracker like Chris Colt."

She giggled.

The door of the Powell House flew open, and a young woman came rushing in, tears running down her cheeks. She just seemed to lose her composure when she saw Chris Colt. He couldn't figure out what was going on as she ran right up to him. He rose and wrapped his arms protectively around the young woman as she threw herself against his chest, sobbing. The waiter handed a clean napkin to Chris Colt, who in turn, handed it to the woman. She dabbed at her eyes as she tried to regain her composure. Once she had, she acknowledged Charley with a nod and a forced smile.

"Oh, Mr. Colt," she said, "I took the stage up Oak Creek Grade and was headed to your ranch. I spotted your famous horse in the livery stable and asked around. I am so grateful to the good Lord that you are here!"

Colt said, "Thank you, but I don't understand."

"I'm sorry. My family sent me to fetch you, sir. Everyone says that you are the one man who can help us. Please—you must."

Chris said, "Fine, but what is it, ma'am?"

The woman sat down by Charley, trying to steel herself against crying. She was young, maybe still in her teens, with blond hair poking out from underneath her sunbonnet.

"You know this late spring storm that came upon us, Mr. Colt? Well, the other day my sister, Sarah, and our brother, Lucifer, took a hike up a trail off Oak Creek Grade. The one that goes up to Tanner Peak. You know the trail?"

Chris nodded his head.

She continued. "The storm came in, and we never heard from them since. Oh, Mr. Colt, my little sister is only eight years old! But Lucifer is fifteen and was raised to hunt and fish by my father and uncle. I know they have to be alive—if only you can just find them."

"Did you get a hold of the sheriff?" Colt asked.

"Yes, that's why I'm here. There is a very incompetent deputy in charge who doesn't believe that they're alive and is quite frankly a buffoon, sir. That's why they sent me to find you. You must help save my little sister and my brother. Please?"

"Of course," Colt said.

Looking at Charley, Colt said, "Send somebody to Man Killer's ranch and tell him to watch for any responses from the telegraph. I'll be home when I get there."

"Sure, Chris. Don't worry. I'll handle everything," Charley said, then hugging the young lady, she tried to soothe her. "Don't you worry. My brother will find them, and they'll be okay."

Colt threw a wad of bills across the counter and was out the door, holding the young woman's arm, before the waiter could even answer.

He took her to the stage station and put her on the same stagecoach from which she had just disembarked and sent her back toward Canon City, promising to meet her there. The sun was now shining and all was bright, the ground very muddy.

Before she boarded, Colt said, "Don't you worry. You'll see me tomorrow morning. I'll be up on Tanner Peak, probably spend the night there."

Colt ran to the mercantile to resupply himself, buying some warm clothes to wear. He had War Bonnet saddled and was on his way down Oak Creek Grade within fifteen minutes.

Famished, Charley decided to order a plate of lobster and enjoy a good meal. When she finished her lunch and started to leave, the telegrapher came in the door in a hurry.

"Miss Colt," he said, excited, "I heard you and your brother were in here, but he left quickly."

Charley nodded.

The clerk went on, "Well, this telegram came in for him right away, ma'am."

Charlotte read the telegram from a marshal in Pagosa Springs, which read that the marshal had indeed stopped the young Ute warrior because he was acting suspicious in town, but he had to let him go because the mount didn't have the Coyote Run or Colt brand on it yet. The telegram stated that the warrior headed west in the direction of Ignacio.

Charlotte pulled two double eagles from her purse and placed them in the telegraph clerk's palm. His eyes opened wide with enthusiasm.

"This is very important," Charley said. "You must get word to Mrs. Wanamaker at my ranch and tell her to watch the children and cook the meals, and you must send a messenger to Man Killer's ranch and tell him all about the marshal's telegram. Let them know that I am going after the horse thief, because Chris is tied up and time is of the essence. It is over one hundred and fifty miles to Pagosa Springs. I'll take the rails and rent a horse once I'm there."

The clerk nodded, saying, "Yes, ma'am. I got it all."

Charlotte bought some quick supplies and hopped on the next stage to Alamosa. From there, she would take a train west.

The next morning, the young lady who had come into the restaurant ate breakfast with her family at the covered wagon they had driven to the trailhead along the Oak Creek Grade stage road.

Her name was Brooke Rudd, and her father, Aaron, was a tall strapping man with work-toughened hands, wind-tanned skin, and a set of arms and shoulders that obviously would make most things that he grabbed a hold of move. He was related to Anson Rudd, one of the founding fathers of Canon City, and was a cousin of Brandon Rudd, Chris Colt's dashing and very sharp attorney, and close friend. Brandon was there eating as well, but now had red eyes rimmed with very dark circles from lack of sleep.

Aaron broke the silence of the meal, saying, "Brooke, I thought you said that Colt would be here this morning."

Brandon interrupted, "He will if he said so."

Seconds later, one of the little boys on the wagon yelled, "Look!"

They looked up the trail and saw Chris Colt riding down from the mountain. He rode up to the wagon, nodding hello to Brandon. Colt dismounted and walked over to the coffeepot. After pouring a cup and drinking from it, he gave a long shiver, and walked over to Brandon.

Chris noticed Brandon's haggard appearance and sarcastically said, "Looks like you been taking good care of yourself."

Brandon chuckled.

Colt said, "What's yer stake in this, Brandon?"

The lawyer said, "They're my cousins, Chris, and we're all very close. You have to find them."

"I'll do my best," Colt said. "Tell me all about them."

After introductions were made, Colt was offered breakfast while they related to him information about the two family members and their experience in the wilds, as well as particular interests or strengths that each child had.

Finally, Aaron said, "Colt, I wanna know how you were able to get past us this morning to go up the trail?"

Colt said, "I didn't. You know the trail that starts off heading this way up at the very top of Oak Creek Grade? I came down the Grade last night, and went up that trail and had a look around on top. I camped up on Tanner Peak and just came down to let you know I'm here."

A voice made all eyes turn. "Mr. Colt, we're glad you're here to help out, but I got everything under control. Can I meet with you in our tent yonder?"

Chris Colt looked at the man who spoke. A Fremont County deputy sheriff's badge glinted on his roughed-out leather vest. The man had oversized homespun trousers, a faded blue shirt, and an ample belly hanging over his belt. His black teamster boots were pulled up over the outside of the trousers and were very dirty and scuffed. The thing that irritated Chris Colt right away was the look of arrogance on the man's bearded face.

"Excuse me," Colt said to the family, and then he followed the deputy to a large tent. Once inside, a gruff, dirty little man handed the deputy a cup of coffee from a pot belly stove. There was a large map of the area pinned to the wall of the tent and several people sat at a long crude table set up on barrels.

The deputy stuck out his hand and said, "We haven't met, Mr. Colt. My name is Deputy Sheriff Wilbur Roy. I am in charge of this search operation."

Colt shook hands saying, "I know most of the deputies around here. You must be new."

"Yeah," the deputy said. "Moved here from Alamosa a few months ago." He walked over to the map, saying, "Let me show you your area of responsibility, Colt."

"My area of responsibility?" Chris echoed.

"Yes, we want you to ride out here toward Florence and check for any possible fires, campsites, or anything like that."

"That area is away from the mountain and toward town. Why would you have me check there?"

"Well, we think there is a chance that there could be an abduction here. We have a teenager and a young child missing, and we have had numerous searchers checking all over the trail they were on. There is absolutely no sign of them. We are suspicious that the children may have been taken somewhere."

Trying to look important, the deputy continued, "Now, it is hard to coordinate a search such as this, so it is imperative, Mr. Colt, that all searchers check in every two hours and let us know how the search is going."

"Right," Colt said and turned for the door of the tent.

The deputy's voice followed after him. "Mr. Colt, where you going?"

Without looking back, Colt said somewhat sarcastically, "To take care of my area of responsibility."

He went back to the family group and sat down at their wagon, where Brandon had a plate of hot food and more coffee ready for him. Between bites, Colt told Brandon what had transpired in the tent.

Brandon said, "Yesterday, one of the local ranchers tried to tell Roy where he wanted to search, and that deputy threatened to arrest him for not obeying a lawful order. What are you going to do?"

"What I think is right," Colt replied. "They are up there somewhere in the deep snow, Brandon. There was no sign of them coming down once the snow started. You have to use your common sense."

"Are they dead?"

"Brandon, they're your family. You want a lot of hope or an honest answer?"

"Your true feelings please."

Colt took a breath and said, "I hope and pray they're both alive, holed up somewhere. Pray for that."

Colt lit a cigarito and offered one to Rudd.

Chris went on. "If the older one was still alive or unhurt, I believe they both would be down here by now. Maybe she knew enough to find shelter and keep a fire going. Don't give up hope. I'm just saying what my common sense tells me."

"What about your area of responsibility?" Brandon asked.

Colt grinned, saying, "I have a terrible sense of direction. I'll probably get lost."

Chris untied War Bonnet and tightened his cinch strap. As he did, a little weasely-looking young man emerged from the headquarters and ran up to Colt. He started to hand Colt a large yellow strip of cloth.

"Make sure you tie this around your left arm," the young man said.

Colt was shocked. "Why?"

"There are a lot of ridgelines and peaks around. This way, at a distance, a searcher won't see you and mistake you for Lucifer Rudd."

Chris chuckled, ignored the strip of cloth, and mounted up in the saddle.

The young man got upset and held the strip up for Colt to take. "I'm serious, Mr. Colt. All searchers are to wear these on their left arms."

Colt looked at him and started roaring with laughter as he wheeled his horse and spurred him up the mountain trail.

It was seven miles from the basic site up to Tanner Peak, which was over nine thousand four hundred feet in elevation. Colt was glad they were right at the edge of the prairie and not in the big range where all the peaks were well beyond ten thousand feet, many over thirteen and fourteen thousand.

War Bonnet was ready to stretch his legs again, so he took off at a canter up the trail. Next to Oak Creek Grade, the trail wound around the edge of a small drainage gully, bounded on the south by a short wall of rock. The trail dipped down into the gully and crossed an intermittent stream. It then started climbing rapidly, switching back and forth on the ridge, but Colt let the big horse have his head. He could tell when the paint wanted to move, and War Bonnet could run other horses into the ground in the mountains.

Chris pulled him back to a trot as the big, long-legged steed made his way up a long ridgeline.

To Colt's left, the terrain dropped down sharply, which was very misleading. At the bottom a steep, rugged stream tumbled down to Oak Creek Grade, where it ran through a large clay and wood culvert. There was very thick scrub oak running down the sides of the hill, choking both hillsides on the side of the stream.

To his right, Colt saw steep cliffs and occasional deer trails, but the trails were so rough very few horses would be agile enough to make it down safely. At some places, there were large outcroppings and at others there were huge trees. The vistas were beautiful, and Colt felt it was a shame he had to be looking for missing youngsters in such pretty environs.

When Colt crossed the saddle of the long ridge, the horse finally started stepping into melting snow. Colt was very concerned because the nights up at that elevation during this time of year were very cold, well below freezing. The temperature in the daytime, however, had been in the seventies down below, and the fifties and sixties up near the peak.

Just before crossing the saddle, Colt finally reached the place where he had found the last sign of the two children before he had come down off the mountain that morning. The tracks had disappeared under the snow, leading upwards. It meant they had to still be up there or they had taken another route off the mountain.

Chris already figured that the pair must be up higher where he now was or where there was still very deep snow. If they had perished, their bodies would be covered by now. If they had come down, even part way, their tracks would have been found by somebody. While he searched, he saw many scouts scouring the landscape, but most of the posse members were following the easiest paths and trails.

Earlier, Colt saw that the children's tracks had been carefree and unhurried, apparently without any idea that a deadly storm was going to blow in quickly. He had found two spots where the youngsters had climbed up on top of some rock outcroppings. It seemed that both were eager to peer at the scenic outlooks. He concluded that they had been having a good time, and being full of adventure, were probably headed all the way up to Tanner Peak.

Next, Colt decided to ride up to the peak and start down from there, figuring that along their adventure, the young pair ran into the snowstorm. That's when they got into trouble.

War Bonnet liked trotting through the snow and tossed his head proudly as he climbed steadily uphill. As he crossed over the other side of the saddle, Colt now had a long ridge running all the way to Tanner Peak on his right. On his left was a very high, rough, steep-sided ridge covered with numerous rock outcroppings and towering pine trees. North Chandler Creek ran down at the bottom of the ravine below Colt. It was here that War Bonnet suddenly stopped and turned back to face a gentle slope that ran down through the trees to the North Chandler Creek below. The big horse's nostrils flared in and out, his ears pricked toward the opening of the gulch.

Colt said, "What are you doing, boy? You never stop like that. You smell a lion or bear?"

Shrugging his shoulders, he turned the horse and continued on the trail, wondering what spooked his sturdy companion. Chris rode for several more miles, winding and climbing until he passed over the top of Tanner Peak. The snow here was over War Bonnet's knees in many places. Colt started down the trail, looking back, trying to put himself inside the mind of Lucifer, picturing the young man in the midst of a blizzard screaming in from over the ridges.

As he slowly descended, Colt got an idea. He dismounted and led War Bonnet down the trail, but as he did, he squinted his eyes tightly, so he could barely see. Doing this, he figured he would simulate the lack of visibility the pair would have had in a total whiteout, visibility limited to only a few inches in front of them.

Where the large ridge over North Chandler Creek ran down across the trail, Chris Colt found what he was looking for. Coming back down the trail, it dropped sharply down right after crossing that ridgeline, and the easiest path from there was to turn right and follow the top of the ridge with visible trees and scattered stands of scrub oak.

On a hunch, Colt ground-reined War Bonnet and got down on his hands and knees. Creeping along the ridge, he found a spot where someone walking would have been naturally funneled between two large blown-down branches. Here, Chris carefully started shoveling snow away with his hands, and as he got closer to the ground, he blew away the remaining crystals. There beneath the snow, he set his cheek on the ground and looked carefully at the indistinct but definite footprints of the two Rudd children. Just as Colt surmised, they had indeed turned off the trail and went along this very same ridgeline.

Colt followed farther along the snow-covered ridgeline. After three-quarters of a mile, Colt came to a rock outcropping directly on top of the ridge. Made up of numerous boulders in a large group, it blocked easy access along the ridge, although a person could walk right over it by maneuvering between boulders. Chris led War Bonnet by the reins and had to stop twice to break branches from a few sparse trees growing among the rocks so that they could continue on unimpeded. Once across the outcropping, the ridge dropped down sharply for a hundred yards then leveled out again.

Colt came across other outcroppings every several hundred yards. Some weren't quite as wide as the first, and he was able to go around them easily. The forested side of the ridge to Colt's left ran down very sharply to North Chandler, disappearing out of sight below. Off to Colt's right was an even steeper drop. Colt could easily see South Chandler Creek, which was much wider than its brother, and its valley much broader.

Chris came to another rock outcropping and spotted a small pine, most of it blackened by a roaring fire. Colt saw the remains of the fire between two rocks down below, ten feet from the scorched tree. The snow had melted away here, and Colt got down on his hands and knees again and placed his face against the ground. He spotted a number of small very faint footprints around the fire. The Rudd children had apparently created the very large fire by building a half teepee of branches up against the apex of where two rocks came together. Their tracks showed that they would get warm at the fire, but then would get too hot and back away, moving forward out of the cold again, over and over. The fire must have been so large, it had scorched the pine from ten feet away.

Colt spoke to his horse. "They were plenty cold when they built that huge fire. The snow must have been blinding then, and they probably didn't want it to put their fire out."

Chris led War Bonnet along the top of the ridge. On the South Chandler side, he spotted something out of place. He stopped the big paint and got his spyglass out from the saddlebags. Colt looked down the slope and saw a set of tracks in the partially melted snow leading up the hillside to the ridge he was on. He squinted through the spyglass and saw that the trail originated near a group of boulders and pine trees down below.

Colt mounted his horse and started down the hillside. It was so steep that Colt had to switchback his horse down the hill, the teardrop stirrups actually touching the ground on the uphill side. Colt passed a couple of glory holes that had been dug into the ridge's base by miners, and soon made it into the grove of trees and boulders where the tracks led. Soon enough, Colt found a bed of fresh pine boughs and another firepit, again built against the apex of two rocks. Just like a signature, the fire had been built the exact same way.

Colt took a stick and jabbed it into the coals of the fire. The ashes were fairly deep, which meant a lot of firewood had been burned. He put his hand into the coals, and noticed they were still warm down in the very center. Colt was not too far behind the children—maybe a half a day, he figured. He looked up through the trees at the giant slope before him. Covered with giant scrub oak thicket, it rose almost straight up for about five hundred feet. People climbing up there in the snow would surely be exhausted by the time they reached the summit.

Colt walked around the grove and noticed that every dry branch he could find had been broken off the trees, apparently used for the fire. The pine bough bed had been slept in, Colt noticed, and he pulled a long blond hair from one of the needles.

Colt now knew what had happened. Lucifer had made this camp to protect his little sister. He left her with as much firewood as he could find, probably tried to go cross-country to get help, figuring that she would not be able to make the journey.

"You poor dumb kid," Colt said aloud wistfully, "you should have stayed put and kept the fire going."

Chris could only hope that somehow they both survived. As he left the campsite to check the tracks leading up the hill, his fears were realized. Lucifer had left large depressions in the snow where he walked up the slope. There were now giant holes in the snow, where the sun had melted back the edges of his tracks. Inside these holes, Colt found the little impressions of Sarah's feet in the dirt. She had tried to follow his trail after the snow had melted, apparently having run out of firewood.

Colt looked up at where the big ridge dipped down in a deep saddle between two peaks. Colt knew that this was the way Lucifer would have headed, expecting to make it back to Canon City six miles away. Bravely but foolishly, the boy took off right in the middle of the blizzard, expecting to save his little sister, and perhaps jeopardizing his own life in the process.

Fighting his way up the oak-clogged, almost vertical slope, War Bonnet seemed to sense the urgency of the situation as well. His nostrils flared in and out, recognizing a human scent different from his master's. Instinctively, he knew it was a female. War Bonnet's ears and eyes were alert and searching, and the horse did not even want a rest break when they made it up on top of the slope. Because of this, Colt let him continue to have his head as he ran along the ridgeline toward the ridge's saddle, Chris having to duck low to avoid overhanging branches here and there. In less than a hundred yards, War Bonnet slammed to a stop and turned his head from side to side. Colt saw the horse's nose testing the wind, his intelligent eyes scanning the terrain all around.

War Bonnet tensed up almost as if he was getting ready to buck. Colt could feel the horse stand rigid like a coiled spring, and the tracker followed the horse's eyes. He was staring down the hill a short distance. It was then that Chris saw Sarah, lying in front of a blown-down log, facedown in the snow.

Chris patted War Bonnet on the neck. "Good job, buddy."

He jumped down and ran to the girl, immediately rolling her over to feel for a pulse. It was faint, but Colt's heart leaped as he realized there was still a chance to save the little girl. In a few more minutes, she might have perished. Colt grabbed her and carried her up atop the ridgeline. He cleared a space and laid her down on his blanket. Chris started dragging branches over and quickly built small fires all around her. Chris knew that as you freeze to death, you go through a period of uncontrolled shaking, then a stage of peace and calm. You get very fatigued and you just want to close your eyes and drop into a sleep from which you never awaken. Sarah was at that phase of hypothermia, her pulse sluggish, her body cold and limp. He had seen people die from hypothermia in the mountains even in the middle of July, so he knew how quickly he had to work.

After Chris got the fires blazing, he removed all her clothing except her underwear and started rubbing the circulation back into her limbs. Colt put on a coffeepot, then sat back and smoked a cigarette, letting the warmth of the fires slowly do their work.

Chris, although a Christian, still believed God appreciated a variety of ceremonies, so borrowing from his red brothers, Chris blew smoke to the four compass points, and then prayed for the girl's safe recovery.

After a tense half hour, the girl started to stir, and ten minutes later, her eyelids fluttered, then finally popped open. She looked at Colt strangely and smiled, then her eyes closed again. Chris gently slapped her across the face and her eyes opened wide and flooded with tears. She sat up holding her cheek and began to sob.

Chris gave her a big hug and stroked her hair, saying, "That a girl. Cry. It will get the blood pumping through your body. Keep crying, sweetheart. You're okay now."

After a few minutes, her sobs subsided, and she leaned back and looked up at Colt's face. She was frightened, despite the gentle look on Chris's face.

"Who are you?" she asked. "Where are we?"

"Sarah, my name is Chris Colt. Your family asked me to find you and your brother. You got stuck up here in a blizzard that blew in quick."

Realization began hitting her as her mind raced. Chris poured her a cup of steaming hot coffee and stirred in lumps of sugar.

"Drink this," he said. "It will help."

She drank, blowing on the steaming liquid. He could tell that her mind was frantically trying to remember what had happened.

"Where's the fire?" she asked.

Chris understood and, pointing toward the edge of the slope, said, "Your camp was down there, maybe four or five hundred feet away."

"Lucifer built me a big fire and left all kinds of wood, but then he left during the blizzard. You have to find him, sir! He has to be about somewhere. He never came back. He must be hurt."

Colt shuddered, though he tried to hide his feelings from the girl. The boy had been gone since the storm began a couple of days earlier. He surely must have perished, Colt thought. But then again, the girl was still alive.

Chris prepared some hot food, and she ate ravenously. Next, he checked her toes and fingers which she said felt like they were burning, and he thought a couple of them had started to get frostbitten. They were certainly not black yet, so he was not going to worry about it.

"Mr. Colt? We have to find Lucifer," Sarah pleaded.

Chris said, "Listen, pumpkin, first I am taking you down the mountain, but I promise I will come right back up and stay here until I find your brother. Fair enough?"

"Oh, thank you, sir! I know you'll find him!"

Chris checked on her clothing, which he had hung on a few branches not far from the fire, and they were already bone dry, as were her shoes.

"Well," Colt said, "get dressed and we'll go see a very happy family."

She grinned, saying, "They'll be even more happy when you find Lucifer and bring him down, Mr. Colt."

Chris cleared his throat, saying, "Pumpkin, I sure hope that's the case. I will try my best to find him, but you should remember how bad that storm was."

Sarah said, "Mr. Colt, you are famous because you are the very best there is. You will find my brother, I just know it. I'm ready to go, sir."

Colt wrapped her in the blanket, then put his big slicker over her bundled shoulders. He sat her up on the front of the saddle, then mounted up. Because the going would be much easier, he could go back up the ridgeline to the main trail, heading back downhill as quickly as the little girl could comfortably stand it.

Colt looked down at Sarah's face, which was barely visible in her big slicker-covered blanket womb.

"Are you warm?" he asked.

"Yes, Mr. Colt. Warm as a biscuit from the oven."

He smiled and kept pushing War Bonnet around the numerous natural obstacles. Once he made the trail, he still had six miles to go down the mountain to where everyone was searching and waiting for news from him. It took a bit over a half an hour.

Everyone saw Chris Colt coming down the trail with a form wrapped up in the slicker and the blanket. Most assumed Colt was carrying a corpse.

Sarah's mother and sister started crying, but Brandon put his arm around them both and softly said, "Now don't go imagining the worst. I bet Colt has one of them alive, and all wrapped up to stay warm."

As he neared, Sarah's mother and sister, both noticed the broad smile on Colt's handsome face. This made them both cry again, but this time out of total relief.

They ran forward sobbing, along with Sarah's

distinguished-looking father, his arms out-stretched, tears streaming down his cheeks. Colt gently handed the little girl to him, and he hugged her mightily, but carefully.

The girl, after being caressed by her family for several minutes, finally spoke. "Ma, Pa, I was way up on that ridge up there. I was almost frozen to death. Mr. Colt saved my life. He built a bunch of fires all around me and got me warm until I woke up, and then he fed me, and . . ."

The mother bawled openly and hugged Colt's leg while he still sat his saddle. The father walked over and stuck out a hand, shaking with Colt while tears fell from his eyes.

Mr. Rudd tried to speak, but the words would not come out. He just nodded thankfully at Colt several times, trying to find the right way to express his gratitude.

Colt said, "It's not necessary. I have a daughter and a son, too. I know how you feel. I have to get back and look for your boy."

"God speed, Mr. Colt." The father's words invigorated Chris as he started to turn the horse back up the mountain, but he found his trail blocked by Deputy Sheriff Wilbur Roy.

Roy's smile was strained as he said, "Congratulations, Mr. Colt. Can I speak with you in the tent, please?"

Chris rode behind the sheriff over to the tent in which the deputy's headquarters was based. Colt dismounted and followed him inside.

Roy suddenly turned, and angrily told everyone in the tent to get out.

Once they were alone, he looked at Chris and seethed. "See here, Colt, that's good you found the girl, but I am in charge of this search, and I assigned others to cover that area. You were supposed to be out to the east. Why weren't you there?"

Colt replied, "I went up on the mountain instead of out on the prairie, you stupid fool, because that's where they were lost, and now I'm about to go back up there and find the girl's brother."

"The hell you will, Colt. You will—"

Roy didn't even see the punch coming. The only thing he saw was the ceiling of the tent as he flew backward. Chris Colt stormed outside the tent while the others just stared, and spotting a water bucket nearby, he picked it up and walked back inside the tent. Colt tossed the water into the face of the unconscious lawman. Roy sat up sputtering and gasping as Colt snatched him by the lapels.

The deputy stammered, "Why you! You're going to—"

The next punch sent Roy flying off his feet, crashing into the wall of the tent where the map was pinned.

Chris yanked him up again while Roy shook his head, trying to clear the cobwebs.

"What do you suppose is going to wear out first, sheriff—my fist or your jaw?" Colt asked.

"Colt, you better not hit me again. You are already in a lot of trouble."

Colt pulled him close to his face, his teeth clenched, and said, "Listen to me, you idiot. In case you haven't figured it out yet, I'm probably the worst person in the world to threaten. Number two, I have forgotten more about finding people than you'll ever know about it. Number three, I am an amigo of your boss and every other law enforcement officer in the territory. So shut up and let me go find the boy. You can even have all the credit and you'll be a hero. But understand this, Deputy Roy—do not treat me with disrespect ever again."

Colt shoved him down in a chair and noticed the man was visibly shaking. Chris shoved a cigarito in Roy's mouth and lit it, then lit one for himself.

Chris stared at the man and blew smoke in his face, saying, "Now, you shut your mouth, relax, smoke your cigar, and sit around here looking important. I'm going up to find the boy. Any questions?"

The deputy just nodded and quietly said, "No, sir."

"Good," Colt said and walked out of the tent.

Brandon accompanied Colt back to the trail. Chris mounted up and stared at the daunting mountain, then said, "Brand, sometimes I just can't believe the people I have to deal with."

Brandon laughed and then became serious, offering Colt his hand, which Colt accepted.

"Chris, thank you," Rudd simply said.

Colt winked, saying, "My job's not done yet, partner. Your nephew's still up there." He wheeled the horse and took off up the trail, waving over his shoulder.

What had he bitten off this time? he thought. First of all, another frigid night would soon be closing in, and he had another seven miles ride uphill before he could even start looking for the boy.

Fortunately, War Bonnet sensed the importance of the mission, and did not act hesitant or tired, even after the long journey from which they had just returned. The horse seemed even more eager, as the trail was now familiar territory to him.

Colt rode War Bonnet to the same spot on the

ridge where the big horse had stopped earlier, facing back toward the narrow slope leading down into the gulch.

"You've never acted like this before, boy," Chris said. "Might as well go down there and make camp on the stream, anyway. It's almost dark and getting chilly."

The bottom of North Chandler gulch was still covered with patches of snow, and the water was fast-running. But the stream was narrow, only two or three feet wide and a foot or two deep in most places. Chris rode uphill a little ways and soon came to a fairly fresh lion kill. Immediately, his eyes searched uphill on the ridge to his left. He knew that mountain lions would kill a deer, feeding on it, then lying down uphill nearby to keep an eye on it.

Colt, of course, knew the lion would remain unseen and hidden from view, but that never kept him from looking. The lion would return to the deer carcass and feed on it until it started to spoil, then abandon it in search of fresh prey. Less finicky predators like bears, coyotes, buzzards, and crows would take care of the rest of the carcass.

Deciding not to disturb the kill site any more, Chris turned and rode downstream, and soon found himself at the base of the draw where he figured the young man would have crossed. His eyes caught sight of a faint trail where someone had come down from above. The environment had been only slightly disturbed, and most men, even the most seasoned of scouts, would have missed it. But not Chris Colt.

He rode over to the trail and got off the horse to study the ground, dropping down on all fours. Colt immediately found the faint tracks of the fifteen-year-old where he had come down the slope and turned right, heading downstream. Then he saw something that really disturbed him: the fresh tracks of a large grizzly, apparently following the young man's trail.

Colt pulled out his Peacemaker and held the barrel down across one of the bear's front paw tracks, measuring the width of the track. It was over seven inches across the pads.

He looked up at War Bonnet saying, "Big one, buddy. Real big—well over six hundred pounds."

The gulch dropped rapidly along the North Chandler Creek headwaters. It was very steep on both sides. The further down Colt rode, the harder the terrain was for the big horse to navigate. There were also thick stands of undergrowth and large boulders along the stream bottom. The young man's trail, as well as the bear's, continued along the right side of the watercourse.

Chris came to a large rock outcropping that provided a natural overhang to the bank. He dismounted and started making a campsite, first gathering a great deal of firewood in case a storm blew in during the night. He built a fire and fixed supper, then went to bed immediately, planning to be fed and back on the track when the sun came up. Colt thought about the large bear and offered a long prayer, asking for a miracle that he would find the young man alive the next day. He drifted off while praying.

Chris's snooze was interrupted by the sounds of rustling foliage. His eyes snapped open and scanned the area around him.

Suddenly, with a tremendous roar and a rush, a giant silvertip grizzly shot from the thicket on the uphill side of the trail. This monster stood over eight feet tall on its hindlegs and weighed well over a ton and a half.

A grizzly bear, on level ground, could outrun a race horse in a short distance, and this big beast was no exception. He closed the distance between the thicket and him in seconds, and Colt barely had time to spin and fire from the hip, his bullet taking the bruin in the front of the left shoulder with little or no effect.

The bear slammed against the rib cage of War Bonnet, his teeth gnashing, a roar emanating from deep in his chest that reverberated through the canyon like a mighty avalanche. Colt flew sideways, and the horse rolled once and bolted. The bear stopped and stood on its hindlegs, nose testing the wind, while he swung his giant head from side to side.

The bear dropped to all fours and faced his small-sized intruder again. Chris raised his pistol, aiming at the bear's face. The bruin charged, and Chris fired, the bullet glancing off the bear's skull, creasing along its head. It was as if it had been whacked with a fly swatter. The bear slammed into Colt and only his pistol saved Chris from the beast's mighty teeth and jaws as the bear bit down, mangling the forged steel.

Colt pulled his horn-handled Bowie knife from the beaded sheath on his left hip and switched it to his right hand, facing the shaggy killer. The bear stared at Colt through his little beady eyes, while heavy breaths puffed out between its spike-sized teeth.

Colt felt no fear. Yes, the bear weighed hundreds of pounds more than Colt and stood almost two feet taller. He could pick up boulders like twigs, and with his mighty forelegs, excavate an entire hillside just to dig out a tasty marmot. The scout, however, was a true warrior, and he was now staring death in the face. He was conditioned not to feel fear until the combat was over. His head was clear. His nerves were steady. Adrenaline coursed through his body, and he was prepared to match his wits and strength against this superior foe to the end. He knew the odds, but he felt that he could not be defeated.

With a roar like Satan unchained, the bear charged. Colt stood his ground, and the mammoth furry body slammed into Chris with tremendous force, but Colt fell backward and let the bear pass over him. Striking upward with all his might, Colt thrust the Bowie into the bear's chest just behind its left front leg.

With an agility that seemed incredible for its size, the grizzly changed directions in midair, gave a loud roar, and twisted its body at the same time, biting at the knife, which was buried to the hilt in its chest.

Colt opened his eyes and sat up with a start. His head swam, and he looked up at his horse. Colt was breathing heavy and shaking. War Bonnet stood over him, pawing the ground, its nostrils flaring. Chris smelled rotten carrion. He had been dreaming, having a nightmare about that bear attack so many years earlier. Colt shook his head, looking at War Bonnet and the rock overhang above him.

Colt reached for his pistol, and drew it out. His hand went for his Bowie knife, and he gave it a reassuring pat.

He got up, relieved his bladder after holstering both Peacemakers, and started striking camp. Colt added wood to the fire and poured coffee. Colt decided on a cold breakfast of buffalo jerky and hardtack. It was still very dark now, just before dawn, the darkest time of the night.

The carrion smell passed, so he knew the bear was upwind or had checked him out and gone on. Chris pictured the young man half-eaten and half-buried somewhere by the bear. He now knew what had caused the dream. Subconsciously, he had heard or smelled the grizzly prowling around, and it caused him to have the frightening dream about the grizzly attack in Idaho, years before. Colt smiled, knowing he had his mind programmed to protect him from ever being attacked by another bear. Once was enough.

With the sun just starting to peek over the prairie, Colt walked in front of War Bonnet, leading him with one rein. Normally, the horse would walk behind Colt, but with a big bear nearby, Chris didn't want to take a chance. War Bonnet was loyal and smart, but he was first and foremost a horse. If he smelled or saw a bear, he would probably panic and run, especially after having been attacked by one before.

Colt had to find the young man, who he had just about accepted was dead now. But Chris had to bring closure for himself, the family, and the other dedicated searchers who were trying to help find the two lost kids. Colt kept a close eye on his backtrail, feeling several times that the big bear was watching him, even stalking him.

The gulch got even rougher as Chris kept on. It was still dark enough that he had to light matches sometimes to find the old tracks. They were very light, because the boy had been walking on snow when he had made them. The gulch narrowed, in some places only twenty feet across. Where it opened up, Chris could look up the slope to his left and beyond the scrub oak thickets and boulders. He knew the trail started up there, leading down from Tanner Peak.

Colt went another mile, and by then the sun was out. Hearing a noise just around the bend, he moved on cautiously. Colt got closer and suddenly heard the roar of the bear. Chris yanked his rifle from its scabbard and went on slowly. As he went around a large rock out-cropping in the trail, he spotted the big bear on its hind legs, snapping its jaws and roaring in anger. A flaming stick was being shoved out from under the rocks at the bruin, and Chris's heart leapt into his throat.

He lifted the rifle skyward and fired, hoping to scare the bear off, but the grizzly simply turned to face him.

Colt said softly, "Just go away. Don't do it, buddy. This time I'm ready for you."

The bear dropped down to all fours and made his charge. Colt held his aim steady on the left front shoulder of the bear, leading him slightly because of the beast's incredible speed. Colt squeezed off the shot, and the bullet slammed through bone, breaking the shoulder. The bear nose-dived into North Chandler Creek, somer-saulting, but still coming up running and roar-ing. Colt's second shot landed in between the bear's head and shoulder, right through its heart. It went down and skidded to a stop, stone cold dead, just fifteen feet from Chris Colt's boots.

Colt gave War Bonnet a reassuring pat on his shoulder and led the snorting horse around the dead bear. Colt still had his rifle cocked as he gingerly touched the bear's unmoving eye with the end of the barrel. It didn't move. Colt breathed a sigh of relief.

Chris now let go of the rein, tossing it up over the horse's back, and he ran forward to the overhang. There, lying on a bed of pine boughs next to a roaring fire was Lucifer Rudd, his legs looking lifeless, covered with dried blood. He was also sporting a very large black eye.

Colt said, "Your sister is safe."

The boy, who looked weak and gaunt, just welled up with tears. He sobbed for a few seconds and whispered, "Sorry."

Colt pulled out his skillet and food containers and said, "Not necessary. Don't blame you a bit, son."

Chris started making them breakfast as the young man explained, "I was trying to get to Canon City to get help, and I fell off that cliff up there. I hit my eye, and I think I broke both legs. I never got knocked out though."

"How many times did the bear come around?" Colt asked.

"That was the third time, but I couldn't hardly sleep for worrying about it. The fire helped keep him away pretty good," Lucifer said.

"Well, we'll check those legs after you eat and drink a bit. They've waited this long."

145

"Thank you, sir. My name's Lucifer Rudd."

Chris grinned saying, "I know. The whole town's been searching for you."

The young man seemed shocked, then smiled, pleased with this news.

Colt stuck out his hand and shook with Lucifer, saying, "My name's Chris Colt."

Lucifer's eyes opened wide in wonder and awe.

"You're Chris Colt?"

Colt nodded.

The boy sat back, hands folded behind his head, and grinned at the rock overhang above him. He soon drifted off into a deep sleep, so Colt let breakfast cool off while he went to carve as much bear meat as he could, along with the beast's hide, and claws.

When Lucifer awoke two hours later, it was to the smell of the bacon and coffee Colt was reheating on the fire.

Colt said, "I figured you might need a little shut-eye. So while you slept, I made a present for you."

Colt has used the point of his knife to drill a hole through one of the massive grizzly claws, and he had run a thong through it. He slipped the necklace over the youngster's head. Lucifer seemed very proud of it, and admired it all through breakfast. He ate everything Colt fixed for him.

Chris checked the lad's legs, seeing that the tibia and the fibula, the two lower leg bones, were indeed broken. None of the bones punctured the skin, but they would need to be set by the doctor, and maybe need to be rebroken first. Colt set the bones as best as he could, wrapping oilcloth around each leg, then he placed two stout sticks on the side of each leg. He tied them in three places, top, bottom, and center.

After striking the camp, he lifted the young man onto his horse and led War Bonnet back a mile to where the slope was slightly more gentle up Tanner Trail. Colt was sweating by the time they reached the trail, and the boy told him that he was light-headed. Chris lifted him out of the saddle, laid him on his back, and placed his legs on a trailside boulder, leaving them there until the blood drained back into the lad's head. Once his color was back, Colt sat him against the rock. Knowing he was in severe pain, Colt found two long aspen saplings. Chris cut these down and trimmed all the branches off.

He then tied these to War Bonnet's saddlehorn with rope hanging down just below the saddle swells. Next, he used the larger branches, trimmed of sticks and leaves, and fashioned cross-braces across the longer lengths of the travois. He then tied his bedroll across the two sides, forming a large, tight hammock, and laid the young man down on it.

"There," Colt said. "That any better?"

Lucifer looked up, smiling through the pain.

"Yes, sir," he said. "My legs hurt a lot, but this sure helps. I kept seeing a bunch of stars flying around in front of my eyes while I was riding the horse."

"You let me know if that happens while you're on the travois," Chris said.

"Yes, sir."

Colt gingerly mounted up, the long poles of the travois extending under his legs and out past the horse's front shoulders. They then headed down the mountain.

Man Killer ran up to the base headquarters on his big sweaty Appaloosa and slid to a stop beside Rudd's wagon, frightening several searchers who had no idea who he was. Brandon Rudd did, however. The Rudd family had placed a large table by their wagon and were all sitting down to lunch. They were excited because Sarah had been brought out earlier in a buggy by her mother and the doctor, and was pronounced to be in pretty good shape, considering what she had been through. He warned that her toes and part of her feet would burn when they got cold, because of possible tissue damage from frostbite, but she was otherwise pretty healthy.

Brandon looked at his famous uncle, Anson Rudd, one of Canon City's founding fathers, along with local notables James Clelland, and Jonathan A. Draper. These three men were some of the most successful and most highly respected men in southern Colorado, and here they were, seated at his table, eating a meal with little appetite and hoping for a miracle. Now Man Killer was here, too, a legend himself while another living legend was up on the mountain looking for a lost young man with the same last name, the same blood, as Brandon.

Brandon thought back to one of his first dinners with Anson, and the importance of family was brought home to him by the recitation of a poem on the subject by his uncle way back then.

After the dinner was over, Brandon had accepted a fine cigar from his uncle and listened with fascination as the white-bearded man recited the poem he had written himself, entitled "Our Wives and Children."

Our wives and children, precious terms that
   move
And thrill our being with a sacred love.
Divine afflatus! from our inmost souls
It wells and bubbles, every sense controls;
Exalts and purifies, refines, restrains:
It soothes our sorrows, modifies our pains;
Subdues our passions, lifts our souls above
Earth's sordid pleasures to elysian love.
In fact earth's joys would fade and round us
   gloom
As deep and dark as in the silent tomb
Would gather, till life's brightest beams would
   seem
The horrid phantom of some troubled dream.
If 'twere not for these precious gems to light
And cheer our pathway thro' this earthly night.
God bless our wives, first, last, best gift to man,
The crowning beauty in creation's plan;
Our guiding star that points to heav'n above,
Where all is joy and harmony and love.
Our children, also, sparks that scintillate
From love's bright realm where forms ecstatic
   mate.
May they be spared to cheer our varied lives
As we go journeying heavenward with our
   wives.

After the recitation, everyone applauded
heartily.

"Good cigar, Brandon, isn't it?" Anson Rudd Jr. had asked him afterward.

Brandon took a long puff and blew a long slow stream of blue smoke at the engraved copper ceiling.

He smiled and said, "That it is, cousin. That it is."

After the cigars, Anson Jr. excused himself as Mrs. Rudd brought two small snifters of brandy.

Anson Rudd handed one to Brandon and kept the other himself, clipping and offering Brandon another cigar, lighting another for himself.

Dipping the unlit end of his cigar into the brandy, then puffing on it grandly, he said, "I prefer not to imbibe in front of Junior. He has such strong reservations against the partaking of alcoholic beverage, but I feel a small snifter helps take the chill from the night air. Don't you agree, nephew?"

Brandon said, "Yes, sir, I do, and it's a fine liquor, I might add."

"Ah, yes," Anson replied, "imported, and a good year."

Anson went on, "James Clelland is a Scotsman by heritage, emigrating from Glasgow some years back. After a number of successful business ventures elsewhere, he settled in Canon City in 1871. He is a man of great import and keen insight into matters of business and shrewd investing. He is far superior to others in executive ability, and is noted for such."

He took a puff, a dip, and a sip, and continued, "Mr. Jonathan A. Draper is another, dear nephew. One of our earliest and finest citizens. A man of superior business acumen, he stands as one among the foremost in matters of public enterprise. His foresight and keen investing have enabled Mr. Draper to be one of the holders of some of Canon City's finest architectural masterpieces, including his own home."

"Should I meet these men, sir?" Brandon asked.

Anson had told him that he definitely should. That had all been some few years before, and now Brandon looked across the table at these men, who were both clients of his and had added quite a few coins to his own coffers because of their several business dealings.

Brandon himself had become quite successful and was still a relatively young man. But now, he sat there himself feeling helpless, but still slightly hopeful. The one thing he knew was that it was foremost in all of his family members' heads to never, ever give up. Plus, his cousin had an uncommon amount of intelligence and common sense for a man of fifteen years. And he knew if anyone in the world could find him quickly, it would be Chris Colt.

Man Killer walked over, sitting down by Brandon.

He said, "I am not going to stay here. I think I will ride up and look for Colt. Last night, I had a dream he was in much trouble with a bear, and it was very real."

"But you know Colt better than anybody. You know he'll handle a grizzly," Brandon replied.

Man Killer said, "Yes, that is why I have been sitting here with your family, but I was there when he became blind from a grizzly, and remember what happened last year when he was wounded in Kansas?"

Brandon nodded. "I agree, but what are the chances of any bear ever besting Colt again?"

Man Killer laughed and said, "I will sit here a little bit longer, my friend."

"Are you hungry, Man Killer?" Brandon asked.

The Nez Perce horse breeder said, "Another bear lives inside my stomach."

Brandon smiled and got up, retrieving a plate for Man Killer and handing it to him. Harriet Rudd jumped up and ran over, taking the plate from his hands.

"I will fill your plate, Mr. Man Killer," she said sweetly. "Please stay seated and talk with Brandon. We so appreciate you coming to help."

Man Killer said, "Thank you, Mrs. Rudd. The mighty Colt will find your nephew, and you will need no more help."

"I do pray so," she said. "Mr. Colt has been so amazing in the past. Do you think he can really bring us such a miracle, though?"

Just then, someone yelled, "Look!"

All the family members and helpers in earshot looked up the trail running along the ridge. Better than a half mile away, the big black-and-white pinto could be seen dragging the travois, Chris Colt sitting erect in the saddle.

Lucifer's mother started crying immediately and wailed, "He's bringing his body down. Oh, Dear Lord!"

Man Killer patted Brandon on the arm and ran over to Hawk, taking off up the trail at a dead run. They saw the young Indian appear a few minutes later cutting back and forth, climbing up on the switchback trail. Within a short time, all watched the drama unfold as Man Killer slid to a stop in front of Chris Colt. They could see the two speaking, and soon Man Killer wheeled his horse and rushed back down the mountain.

There were anxious moments as they waited for him to approach. As soon as he got back down, Man Killer walked quickly over to the anxious mother and father, a big smile alighting on his face.

"Your son lives. Colt killed a big grizzly this morning as it was attacking your son, and your son has two broken legs, but bones grow together again."

Lucifer's mother started to faint, but Brandon caught her and laid her in the shade of a nearby tree. Several women tended to her, while the father wept openly and dropped to his knees in grateful prayer.

By the time Chris Colt made it down the mountain and was approaching the group, the word had already gone out. At last, Colt came around the final bend and up over the little hump in the trail. A great cry of joy rang out from the crowd. The family members ran up to the travois and surrounded young Lucifer, and people came over just to touch the leg of the incredible Chris Colt. It was a magnificent celebration.

Colt ignored the cheers and adulation and waved for the doctor to come over. Brandon helped keep everyone back while the doctor neared the travois.

Chris explained, "He fell off about a fifty-foot-high cliff. I set his legs and splinted them, but it seems that the bones in both of his lower legs are broken. He bonked his eye also, but he hit it on a branch, not a rock. Told me he never got knocked out when it happened."

"Splendid, Christopher!" The doctor beamed. "You've done a swell job, but we must get him to town to the hospital with great haste. Let us get some gentlemen to help load him onto my buggy seat."

Colt climbed out of the saddle and picked the young man up in his arms, carrying him to the doctor's buggy. He placed him carefully up onto the seat. The doctor thanked him and immediately left for town, followed by several family members, as well as Deputy Wilbur Roy, now sporting his own black eye, wanting absolutely no part of having to face Chris Colt.

Chris sat down at the table and fixed a plate of food, talking to Man Killer and Brandon.

Man Killer said, "When I was at home, a messenger brought a note to my wife. The marshal in Pagosa Springs spotted the thief and his horse, and Charley left to find them. The thief was headed toward Ignacio."

Between bites, Colt said, "Oh, no. When did she leave?"

"Jennifer said that Charley left to take the train right after you left to come here," Man Killer said.

"I have to go help her now. Want to go?" Colt asked.

Grinning, Man Killer said sarcastically, "No, I want to sit on my porch and watch the leaves grow on the trees in my yard."

"Good, we'll take off as soon as I'm done eating," Chris said.

Anson walked up to them and shook hands with both men.

He said, "Mr. Colt, as usual this community is deeply in your debt, but this time, my family is even more so. I am going to host a grand party forthwith, and we would love to have you as guest of honor so we can shower you with praise and gifts. Do you accept, sir?"

Chris replied, "Thank you, Mr. Rudd, but I'm afraid Man Killer and I have to leave immediately and try to find my sister, who is off on a dangerous adventure."

While Chris Colt was searching for the children, Charley Colt, riding a big black bay gelding from a livery stable in Pagosa Springs, showed up in Ignacio. She asked around and was soon hot on the trail of Jimmy the Horse Thief.

From Ignacio, she had to head west, hearing that Jimmy was near Red Mesa, a few miles north of the New Mexico border. Charley picked up the tracks of the horse's bar shoe on the old wagon road she followed to Red Mesa. She grew concerned, though, because tracks of three other riders soon came in from the north and rode over the top of the bar shoe tracks. The bar shoe trail was fresh, so these men, she figured, must have been within earshot.

Charley Colt, in those days, was arguably the most beautiful woman in the entire state of Colorado. Even wearing a man's bib shirt, kerchief, dungarees, and six-shooters, she still could not hide her femininity. Her hair looked like it had been dipped in golden honey. Her piercing blue eyes were intelligent and held an ever-present wisp of a smile, just like her brother's. Her cheekbones were high, and her lips were full, almost making her look like she was pouting. Her teeth were white and even, and to add an even more startling contrast, she spent many hours in the sun, work hardening and toning her muscles, giving her body a dark coppery tan. But what was most catching, even from a distance, was the way her body filled men's clothing with curves that no man could ever supply.

This did not go unnoticed by the three men who were now hiding around the next bend in the dark timber. Ruby Jackson was a former slave who had joined the owlhoot trail as soon as he left the South. Big Ears Eberling was a massive man who was the son of a brothel madam named Two Moons Eberling, a Paiute Indian who got caught up in the bad side of white society, and a customer who was obviously of African heritage. But Two Moons was never sure. The third was Horace Hogan, who was a simple big dumb blonde who did whatever he was told by the other two.

All three had spotted Charley Colt while checking their backtrail, a regular habit that had kept them ahead of more than a few posses in the past. Leering at her through dirty binoculars made their hearts race. A ravishing beauty, unescorted, miles from help and miles from any lawman, was to them like a dream come true. They had plans for Charley Colt, and those plans did not include her ever leaving the dark forest from which they now emerged.

All three had their guns drawn as she came around the bend. Charlotte immediately reined to a stop, her heart thumping as she assessed the characters in front of her. She knew she would have to act fast and keep calm or she would die right there. Mentally, Charley spoke to herself saying, *Keep calm. Breathe slow. Relax your neck and back. Don't show fear. Shoot straight, Charlotte. You're a Colt.*

Charley wrapped her shapely leg around the saddle horn and leaned her right arm across her thigh. Though it was a suggestive maneuver, it also disguised her left hand, which now gripped the handle of one of her Colt Navy .36's.

She cleared her throat to cover the sound of cocking the revolver, then said sarcastically, "My, my, all three of you boys need to hold guns at one time on a poor gal like me? I must be one mean-looking road agent."

Big Ears and Horace immediately holstered their guns. Ruby made a sour face, still holding his gun on her.

He spoke, "That ain't it, lady. We just don't see women not wearin' no dresses. We want a nice look-see at what ya got under them clothes. We'll have us a little hoe-down, just the four of us."

Charley felt her spine shudder, but she forced a phony smile, "Well, we're going to have a little dance all right, but it's going to be you three dancing at the end of a rope."

"Get down," Ruby commanded harshly.

Charley stared into his cold eyes and replied very firmly, "My body will be cold and bloody before I let any of you touch me. But I promise you men this. I'm going to kill you first before I die."

Though beautiful, her icy stare and frosty words chilled Ruby right to the bone.

Big Ears interjected, "How you gonna manage to down all three of us, ma'am? Might's well enjoy the party."

There was the unmistakable cocking of a Winchester from the trees behind them as a man's deep voice said, "Naw, I'm gonna enjoy the party, because you and your buddy there are leaving your saddles as quick as Miss Colt empties her pistol into your friend. I haven't practiced with my carbine yet today."

Charley was shocked but pleased as she saw the stranger walk out of the woods. He was very tall like her brothers and as wide at the shoulders, too. He had a look in his eyes that reminded her of Chris.

As they glanced nervously at him, Charley used the distraction and drew both guns, cocking and leveling them at the criminals.

Big Ears snarled, "She's just a woman. Don't

pay her no attention. We need to take *him* out. That's there's Tell Sackett."

Without warning, Charley fired her right-hand gun, and Big Ears screamed, his name soon to be changed to One-Ear Eberling. He clasped a hand to the spot where his left ear had been, blood running down his fingers and across the back of his hand.

All four men looked at Charley in amazement as she flipped her right-hand gun up in the air, switched her left gun to her right with a border shift, and caught the spinning gun, cocking them both and aiming them at the stunned outlaws.

She grinned, saying, "Yeah, I'm only a woman, but at least I own both of my ears."

Ruby turned to Sackett and said, "Did you call her Miss Colt?"

Tell nodded affirmatively.

"And you're Tell Sackett?"

Tell nodded again. Ruby dropped his gun as though he were holding the wrong end of a flaming torch and stuck his hands up in the air.

Sackett directed the other two to shed their guns, then said, "Okay, boys, now your clothes. Your horses are headed south. I sent them that way already. If you can run fast in your bare feet, maybe you can catch them."

Ruby started to protest, but one look at Charley's guns stopped him. In five minutes the outlaws, moaning and groaning were out of sight.

Charlotte walked over to Tell Sackett and shook his hand. "Mr. Sackett, I have heard much of you and your kin before. I can never thank you enough."

Tell bowed, saying, "My pleasure, ma'am. I too have heard nothing but good things about your family."

"But how did you know I was Charley Colt?"

"What I have heard about your family includes your great beauty, ma'am. There was no mistaking you. Give my regards to Chris. We'll cross paths again."

He mounted up, tipped his hat brim, and slowly rode off to the east. Charley watched him go, trying to catch her breath.

She soon mounted up and took off after her quarry, wondering why she felt so flushed.

It was just outside Red Mesa when Charlotte spotted smoke swirling up into the sky from a stand of trees to the south of the wagon road. She swung around to her left, using the trees to shield her approach. Dismounting at the edge of the wood, Charlotte eased forward from tree to tree, her pistol drawn.

Jimmy Blind Elk sat by his cooking fire, roasting a rabbit over a spit made of a green stick laid across two forked branches. The smoke wafted toward her, and it smelled very good. Charley waited, realizing how hungry she was and decided she might as well not waste good food. Jimmy was not alert enough to look her way anyway. He was reaching into a burlap bag and pulling out a potato, which he sliced into a frying pan on the fire, sizzling with bacon grease.

Fifteen minutes later, Jimmy glared at her, his hands tied behind him. Charley pulled off another bite of tender rabbit and smiled with gleaming white teeth.

"I cannot believe that you would steal food away from my mouth," he said.

"I suppose it's okay that you steal away a great horse from my brother, but I can't steal your food," she replied.

"If you untie my hands, you would die by them, woman."

"You may address me as ma'am, not woman."

Jimmy shouted back, "No! You are woman!"

"Fine, You call me woman. I'll call you hungry," Charlotte said.

It only took ten minutes more before Jimmy said meekly, "Can I eat some food, ma'am?"

"Sure," Charley said, and started fixing him a plate.

As she took it over to him, he said, "Please untie my hands." Charley shook her head. "Just one hand, so I may eat?"

Charlotte walked into the trees and returned carrying a twisted bough with several branches shooting out from the main limb. She set it on the ground in front of him so that it provided a makeshift table. Charley then rested the plate between the crook of two of the branches and commanded, "Bend forward and eat."

Jimmy protested, "No, untie me. I must use my hands to eat."

"Suit yourself. Go hungry. We leave in five minutes," Charley said, then turned and started striking camp. The young Ute immediately leaned over and began gobbling food.

As she helped him up onto her brother's horse and started to lead him away, Jimmy Blind Elk worried about his predicament. At first, he was not alarmed; after all, she was just a woman, he thought. Now, however, he had reason to be concerned. She had tied his hands securely behind his back, and he had to hold the cantle of the saddle for balance. She had also securely tied a piggin string around each ankle, so that if he fell out of the saddle for any reason and the horse bolted, he would be dragged upside down underneath the horse. The thought frightened him immensely, and all plans of escape went out the window.

Charley led her prisoner north. This surprised Jimmy Blind Elk, who said, "We do not go east, back to Westcliffe. Why?"

Charlotte replied, "I don't want to carry you for a couple hundred miles. We're going to Durango. Short ride, nice warm jail. I'm sure you'll like it there."

Jimmy had hoped they would travel a long distance so he would have more time to escape, but now he saw it was not going to be.

Jimmy's only hope was that they were still well within the boundaries of the gigantic Ute reservation where he lived. His hopes suddenly became reality when thundering hoofbeats could be heard. They came up out of an arroyo and terrified Charlotte. It was a large party of Utes, around thirty of them, all armed with rifles and bows, and led by a silver-haired chief wearing a double-trailer war bonnet. He had on a light red shirt covered with large white polka dots, a bone hair pipe breastplate, and beaded buckskin leggings and breechcloth. In his hand was a Winchester 1873 decorated with brass tacks and more eagle feathers. The party came up quickly and formed a cordon around Charley and her prisoner. She immediately drew both pistols, as the chief stopped in front of her.

Jimmy Blink Elk smiled broadly, calling out to the chief, "Grandfather!"

The old man gave Jimmy a cursory glance and then stared at Charley, saying, "You have my grandson tied on that horse. Do you think he is a *wapiti* to take home to the cooking fires?"

"No, your grandson is the thief and coward who shot my brother from ambush and stole our horse here," Charley replied.

"Why does a woman chase a thief?"

"Because my brother Chris is too busy, and your grandson here shot my brother Joshua."

"This is not a good thing. It is not woman's work."

Charlotte felt the hairs on her neck bristle, saying, "Have you not heard of Buffalo Calf Road Woman and Walking Blanket Woman of the Lakotah and Cheyenne? They were great warriors."

He thought for a second and said, "This is straight talk, but my grandson not be taken prisoner by a woman. You cut his bonds now."

Charley clenched her teeth and said, "Like

hell I will. Nobody bushwhacks and steals from the Colt family and gets away with it."

The chief looked at her with surprise, saying, "What your name woman?"

"Charlotte Colt," she said proudly.

He said, "Your brothers, who?"

"Chris Colt and Joshua Colt."

"Put away your guns," the chief said.

His tone of voice did not anger Charley, but instead made her feel reassured. She complied and holstered both guns, cautioning him, "They can come out of those holsters very fast, and if I'm to die, some brave Ute warriors who fight against women will die here with me."

The chief did not act as if he had heard a word that the young beauty said. He looked over at his grandson, then at Charlotte Colt. He cocked the rifle as he raised it, and Charley froze in place, hands hovering over her guns, her stomach rising to her throat.

The chief turned and said to Jimmy, "The mighty Colt is a brother to all who carry the pipe and wear the moccasin. You have brought great shame and disgrace to your father, who is my son. Your life came first from my blood, so then I too can take it away and send it back to Mother Earth."

He fired the rifle, and Jimmy, catching the

bullet through the heart, recoiled from the shot, his head slumping forward on his chest, a giant red stain spreading all over his shirt.

The chief said so all could hear clearly, "The sister of Colt always welcome in land of Ute. Family of the mighty Wamble Uncha are brothers and sisters of the Ute. I have spoken."

As he looked at his grandson, Charley saw the incredible pain and sadness in his eyes, but his posture remained stoic as he wheeled his horse and rode away. Two braves retrieved the body, while the rest followed the chief.

Charley headed toward Durango, a short ride north. She would spend the night there and ride the trains back home. Her mind was on Chris, though, wondering where he now was and what he was doing.

It had been a long day, so an hour outside of Durango, Charley decided to go into a deep grove of trees and make camp. She cooked and ate a hearty meal and was asleep by the time her head rested on her saddle, which doubled as a pillow.

Charlotte slept soundly throughout the night, but was startled awake at daybreak at the sound of a gun being cocked close to her ear. She wanted to jump up, but she feigned sleep instead. The voices were familiar.

Ruby said, "Quit fakin' it. Get the hell up outta that bedroll, woman."

Charley knew she was in trouble now. She reached up for her two pistols, hidden under the saddle. They were not there.

"Lookin' fer these, missy?" Big Ears asked.

She opened her eyes and looked at the three outlaws that she and Tell confronted earlier. Big Ears Eberling, a bloody green kerchief wrapped around his head, held her Navy .36's in his hands, taunting her with them. The look in his eyes chilled Charley to her inner core.

Charley rose, saying, "No, I was looking for an ear. Figured there might be one or two lying on the ground somewhere."

Horace laughed until Big Ears scowled at him.

Big Ears walked up to her, his knife pulled. She froze in a paralysis of fear, her mind racing for a plan of escape. He backed her up to a tree with the knife. Charley kept wanting to grab his wrist, but she reasoned that he was just too big and strong. She would have to wait and survive, watching for another chance. Big Ears suddenly sliced straight down with the blade, which he had been holding at her throat. It cut through her blouse and undergarments and Charley's breasts fell free. Horace cleared his throat, and Big Ears whistled, then chuckled menacingly.

Charley held her breath, covering herself with crossed arms.

"Back away," Ruby commanded. "Her name is Colt, remember? She's worth a lot a money, but not damaged."

Big Ears stood his ground, not taking his eyes off her hands, which just covered the ends of her ample breasts.

He said, "She's payin' fer my ear."

"You want that or part 'a one million dollars?" Ruby asked.

Big ears turned around and stared at Ruby. "You mean it?"

"If she ain't damaged goods. What do ya think the Colts would do if we damaged her, huh?"

Horace finally said, "Yeah, Big Ears, money is one thing. Damaged goods is another."

Big Ears laughed. "What d'ya know, the dummy has an opinion."

Horace laughed stupidly, as Big Ears turned and sheathed his knife.

"You got another shirt?" Ruby asked.

"In my saddlebags." Charlotte replied.

She had hope. Her backup gun, a Colt Russian .44, was in one of the saddlebags. But her heart dropped as Ruby walked over to retrieve it, and he pulled the gun out as he tossed her a clean blouse. He even made Big Ears and Horace turn while she changed shirts. Ruby then tied her hands with her own piggin string.

"Saddle her horse, Horace," Ruby commanded, "we got to hurry and marry up with the others. We'll have ta take her with us."

Charley said, "Where are you taking me?"

Ruby grinned, saying, "Ever been to Utah?"

CHAPTER 6
On the Job

Numerous Canon City residents and members and friends of the Rudd family came up to thank and shake hands with Chris Colt. This made the tracker uncomfortable, so he held his plate and walked into the nearby trees with his close friends. Colt finished his food, then the three men—Colt, Man Killer, and Brandon Rudd—shook hands and the duo left, just like that. Instead of heading back up Oak Creek Grade, they decided to head up Grape Creek, following it all the way up to the Wet Mountain Valley several miles south of the ranch.

They stopped to rest the horses atop the flat grassy area between Curly Peak and Tanner Peak. As they let the two horses take a breather, they dismounted and smoked cigarettes.

Chris looked at a big cottonwood with low thick branches at the edge of the park.

He nodded at it and said, "Remember when that cur Wolf Keeler was after you and that grizzly mauled you? Did I ever tell you what happened to me, when I was looking for you?"

Man Killer said, "You just said you had a run-in with Keeler and his posse of bad men."

"I had a run-in all right. They not only tried to hang me, but they tortured me in the process."

"They tried to hang you?" Man Killer said.

Colt looked at the big cottonwood and thought about that frightening day and told Man Killer what had happened.

Wolf Keeler, a crooked deputy from Westcliffe, had said, "See ya around, Colt. Hope that horse a yours has plenty of stay to him. C'mon boys, let's find the red nigger."

He was referring to Man Killer, whom the posse had been after. Man Killer and Colt were to be eliminated under the orders of Keeler's real boss, an evil mine owner named Preston Millard.

Colt simply said, "Mister, you just made a big mistake."

Wolf Keeler laughed aloud and slapped his horse with the reins. The posse followed Keeler back up the gulch and left Chris Colt standing there on the back of War Bonnet, hands tied behind his back, noose around his neck tied to a low hanging cottonwood branch. If the horse would have moved just a foot or two, Chris Colt would have been strangled to death. He even thought about kicking the horse so he would fall off and snap his neck, dying more quickly, but there was no quit to Chris Colt. He had to figure a way out of this without giving up.

Chris spoke softly, "Steady, boy. Stand, War Bonnet."

His mind worked quickly, calmly, and methodically. Chris Colt had gotten himself out of near-death situations before by thinking his way through them, but this seemed darned near impossible.

He kept speaking softly to his now nervous paint horse. "Easy, boy, easy," Chris said.

He could tell that the scent of a mountain lion or bear was on the wind by the nervous way War Bonnet was now prancing and tossing his head around. His nostrils flared in and out, and he whinnied nervously.

"Stand, War Bonnet. Easy, boy."

Colt got an idea. He kept talking softly to his horse and walked back onto the horse's rump. This really made War Bonnet nervous. Chris remembered a trick he had been teaching the horse, and he prayed now that the horse would remember the trick, as well.

Colt, still on War Bonnet's rump, bent his knees and said, "War Bonnet, Kick!"

The horse's hindquarters rose high in the air as he kicked with both feet. At the same time, Chris Colt jumped and bent his body forward landing, stomach-first, on top of the branch. Colt lay there on the branch, tears in his eyes, and he breathed a heavy sigh of relief. He uttered a prayer of gratitude as he caught his breath. War Bonnet pulled peacefully at some mountain grasses down below.

After hearing the story, Man Killer grinned, saying, "You were very smart. You might have died that time."

Colt lamented, "Man Killer, do you miss the days of scouting for the cavalry, and all the battles?"

Man Killer smiled. "Great Scout, you worry that you will no longer feel alive just tracking, but you will. Badge or not, cavalry or not, you will always be Chris Colt. People will always want you to be Chris Colt."

Colt smiled and the pair mounted up, moving on toward home. They decided that they would resupply at the ranch, then flag down a train after fording the Arkansas. From there, they would take the rails to wherever Charley was, giving the horses a chance to rest.

It was after dark when both men arrived at the Coyote Run. The horses were tired and so were Colt and Man Killer. They rubbed down both steeds, gave them some oats, corn, and fresh alfalfa mixed with grass.

Colt said, "I'd like to spend the night and sleep, but I want to find Charley as soon as possible. I'm going to eat, then pack and take off."

Man Killer said, "I will be with you, my friend."

They walked up the steps and into the house. The children had already visited them in the barn, and so had Tex briefly. Chris and Man Killer were both suddenly very hungry when they entered the kitchen to the delicious aromas of cooking food. There were several pots and pans on the stove filled to the brim, and there was something baking in both the oven and the Dutch oven.

Colt looked at Man Killer, saying, "I never knew Tex to cook up such a spread when Charley's away."

"Maybe Joshua cooked it," Man Killer said.

Colt looked at Man Killer as though he were crazy, and both men chuckled as they walked into the dining room. There, the children of Chris and those of Charley sat at the table, along with Joshua, Tex, Long-Legged Bear, and setting a casserole pot on a warmer was a woman whose beauty instantly took away Colt's breath. She set the casserole pot down and then seated herself. During the whole time Chris Colt could not take his eyes off of her.

"Chris, Man Killer, I want to introduce you to Miss Amanda Morelli," Joshua said. "Mrs. Wanamaker has a family to tend to and couldn't be here all the time. Mandy was looking for work at the restaurants at Westcliffe, so we hired her to come here temporarily to cook and clean up around here a little bit. At least until Charley gets back."

Chris and Man Killer both got up and shook hands with her, but Chris could not speak. Man Killer was cordial and made polite conversation, while Colt simply stared at her.

Her figure equaled Charley Colt's, and she had an olive complexion, shiny black hair that hung all the way down to the top of her buttocks, and very green eyes. She was almost full-Italian in her ancestry, except for her maternal grandmother, who was a blue-eyed, blond-haired Swede. Everyone figured that's where Mandy's piercing green eyes came from. Her face was classically beautiful, with full lips, a strong jaw, and very high prominent cheekbones. Her nose was slender and straight. Her carriage, even when she walked in with the casserole, was proud, aristocratic, even regal.

People at the table spoke with each other, but Chris Colt wasn't listening. He kept glancing at Mandy, and she caught him looking several times, and he would blush and look away. He could not eat his food.

Joshua looked down the table at his brother and knew something was wrong. Chris Colt, the legendary chief of scouts, who had faced gangs of outlaws singled-handedly, the man who had fought and killed a grizzly with just a knife, and scouted against the likes of Victorio, the hero to all who know of him, just sat at the table, head bowed, tears flooding his eyes.

Joshua was genuinely concerned.

"Is anything wrong, Chris?"

Colt cleared his throat and shook his head almost imperceptibly as he rose and started quickly from the room, quietly saying, "Excuse me."

Colt ran up the stairs, two steps at a time and down the long hallway to his bedroom. He went inside, closing the door behind him, and threw himself across his bed and bawled like a newborn without milk, his face buried in the pillow to muffle the sound. He kept picturing the beautiful young Miss Morelli. It made Colt cry even harder.

After a few minutes, his tears subsided, and there was a light knocking on the door.

"Who is it?" Colt muttered.

"It's me," Joshua replied.

He opened the door gingerly and came in, sitting on the foot of the four-poster bed.

Colt sat up, embarrassed, and said, "Sorry."

Joshua said, "Pshaw! For what? What happened?"

"That woman, Joshua. She is so beautiful. It is the first time I have looked at any woman since . . ." he paused, ". . . since Shirley left, and I feel so damned guilty."

Joshua said, "Chris, you're still a young man, and it has been close to two yeas since Shirley died. You can't stop living."

Colt said, "Well, I did."

Chris suddenly started crying again and punched the pillow saying, "Dammit, Joshua, why did Shirley have to die? Why didn't she just let those kidnappers go?"

"You know why," Joshua said. "She sacrificed her own life to save your children and Charley's. Is this the first time you've gotten mad at Shirley for dying?"

Colt nodded.

"Good," Joshua said, "You've needed to. Get it out of your system. It's good for you."

Chris burst into tears, speaking again, "I'm tired of being Chris Colt. People expect too much from me, Josh."

Joshua smiled. "Maybe you expect too much from yourself. Maybe that's one of the reasons Chris Colt is a legend."

"Would you handle everyone for me, brother?" Colt asked. "I'm going to stay up here."

Joshua got up, saying, "Sure. Get some sleep."

He stopped at the door at Colt's voice. "Joshua, thanks."

Joshua winked and went out the door.

Seconds later, the door opened and Chris sat bolt upright on his bed. Kuli, his pet wolf, ran through the doorway and jumped up on his bed, giving Chris wet licks all over his face. Long-Legged Bear followed.

Colt joked, "You didn't knock."

The old man ignored the remark. Long-Legged Bear gave Colt a serious look for several seconds. Chris didn't know what to make of it and just looked back.

After a pregnant pause, Long-Legged Bear said, "When the great wife of Wamble Uncha decided it was time to walk the spirit trail, she decided to do that so her family would not have to walk the trail yet. You were part of that family."

Colt watched in amazement, speechless as the old man sauntered over to Colt's shirt and extracted a cigar, lighting it on a bedside lantern chimney, and then headed toward the door.

At the door, he turned, saying, "She wanted Colt to live, not die with her."

He had started out the door, when Colt said, "Did God, or Wakan Tanka, or Gitsche Manitou, or Usen, or whatever you call Him. Did he send you to us?"

Long-Legged Bear turned, smiling for one of the first times that Colt had ever seen him, and said, "He sent us all."

He exited the room, closing the door quietly behind him.

Colt lit a cigar and sat by the window in his rocker, petting Kuli and watching the stars.

The next day found the crew getting ready to mend an entire fence line that was knocked down during the night by a harem of elk that spooked because of a coyote. The harem of elk, numbering in the hundreds, was grazing on the lush green pasture when the coyote began chasing a little mouse. So intent on the chase was the canine that he plowed smack dab into the head of one of the herd cows who had her head down grazing. She leapt high into the air and bounded toward the wooded slope in sheer panic. This quickly spread to the other elk around her. The elk, which normally bounded gracefully over the fence, ran into it in blind fright and sent it crashing down.

Long-Legged Bear had proven himself pretty handy with a team, so he offered to drive the freighter wagon, loaded with cold water and carefully cut and trimmed cedar fence posts, wire, and any other tools needed for mending the fence.

Mandy Morelli stayed at the ranch house and waited for the tutor, Mrs. Wanamaker, to show up for her daily sessions with all four children. After the attempted kidnapping on the Colt children the previous year, the Colts decided it would be safer for the children to get the rest of their education at home with their own schoolmarm. Chris had also elected to always leave Kuli at the house to protect Charley and the kids.

Colt and Man Killer were packed up and ready to leave shortly after daybreak, deciding to eat breakfast in Westcliffe. Chris was very nervous as he went up to say good-bye to Mandy.

He could barely breathe when she shook hands with him. Her handshake was firm, and she looked him squarely in the eye, but her hand was so soft. Colt knew that his face must be red, and he noticed Man Killer's slight grin as he moved farther away with his horse.

"Mr. Colt, may I ask you a question?" Mandy said.

"It's Chris, please. And, of course, ask away, Miss Morelli."

"First of all, by the same regard, please call me Amanda or Mandy, sir . . . I mean Chris."

He interrupted, "Which do you prefer?"

"Mandy, but either name is fine," she replied. "I don't mean to be personal, but last night at the dinner table, did I do something to offend?"

Colt almost stammered, "Oh, no, no. Heavens no! You didn't do anything wrong, Not at all. I'm sorry if I gave you that impression."

"Well, it was just that after we were introduced, and you, well, you cried," she said.

Now Colt knew his face was red, indeed.

"Mandy," he said, "I am very sorry that I made you feel bad. Can we go sit on that bench? I'll explain."

She started walking, and he held up a finger

to her, walking over to Man Killer, saying, "Go ahead. I'll catch up."

Man Killer grinned.

Colt let War Bonnet stand where he was, while he walked to the bench overlooking Texas Creek. He sat down beside Mandy.

"How should I start?" Chris muttered. "Mandy, I loved my wife very much. For almost two years, I have not even thought about another woman. None. Do you mind if I smoke?"

She shook her head, smiling sweetly.

He fumbled around and finally found the makings and rolled a cigarette, lighting it while his mind searched for the right words.

"When I met you last night," he said nervously, "I found myself not able to look away."

She blushed, saying, "What do you mean?"

Colt knocked his ashes off the cigarette, and some fell in the crook between his little finger and ring finger, burning it. Colt yelled, "Ow!" and shook his hand.

Mandy chuckled, but then said, "I'm sorry. Are you hurt?"

Embarrassed again, Colt said, "I'll be fine," and stuck his hand in the icy cold water of the stream.

"As I was saying," he continued, "last night, when we met. Well . . . well, your beauty. It is just overwhelming. I mean. I'm sure you hear that over and over, about how beautiful you are."

"No, I don't," she replied innocently. "Nobody ever says that to me."

Colt could not believe it.

"That's preposterous!" he said. "You should be told that every day of your life."

The import of that statement hit Colt as soon as the words left his mouth. He really got embarrassed now and almost ran to his horse, scooping up his reins. He tipped his hat toward Mandy.

"I have to hurry to catch up to Man Killer," he said. "Nice to have you here at the Coyote Run. See you when we return."

She just gave a wave as he launched himself out of the yard on the big paint, but only because she could not speak. Her heart was pounding so hard, Mandy was afraid that her chest was going to explode. She could not breathe. She knelt down and began splashing the icy cold stream water on her face.

Colt spent the next hour catching up to Man Killer on the way to Westcliffe. They arrived in town a short while later with Colt's wise young partner not making any comments about Amanda Morelli.

They went into the main saloon in Westcliffe for a breakfast of steak and eggs, but what they really wanted was information. And a saloon was the best place for gathering it.

Colt spoke with several patrons in the place and learned all the latest. The biggest news was that electric lights had been installed in Denver, and they actually worked. The city already had telephones a few years earlier. It was all pretty amazing to Colt.

Leadville was being talked about a lot because of all the silver being mined there, making so many people rich. It was probably the highest town in the United States at over ten thousand feet elevation, and it now had thirty-one restaurants, seventeen barber shops, fifty-one grocery stores, four banks, and an unbelievable one hundred and twenty saloons.

The other news from around the state was the building of the big irrigation canal near Fort Lyon out east, to start making the prairie land greener and more productive. That was already under construction, and many thought it would make Colorado more wealthy agriculturally.

The news that made Chris Colt's heart leap, however, was hearing about the gang who entered a small town in the Four Corners area and stole a simple Conestoga wagon. A deputy sheriff went after them and was shot to doll rags when he tried to arrest them. It seems that they had stolen a Gatling gun from a cavalry post in Wyoming and broke an axle outside Silverton, but nobody knew why they would even be in that area. Nobody knew why they stole the Gatling gun, either.

The four men had then gone into a brothel near Silverton and two prostitutes ended up horribly disfigured, one lingering near death. They also killed the family of a deputy sheriff west of Durango by shooting them with the Gatling gun, seemingly for practice.

Several posses converged and had chased them into the wild desert of southeastern Utah on the large Navajo Indian reservation right near the Four Corners area. They were somewhere along the San Juan River, which ran through the dry brown landscape like a giant green ribbon. The river bottom area was covered, Colt knew, with manzanita and Russian olive trees, thick enough to hide an army in places, and full of thorns that would cut a man to shreds trying to go through it.

Colt looked across his bite of steak, saying, "You thinking what I'm thinking?"

Man Killer grinned, swallowing his food.

"Her name is Colt, after all," he finally said.

"If something that big happened that close, I believe Charley is there in the fight. She probably wants to take on all the outlaws herself."

The two men went out into the street, and Colt grabbed Man Killer's arm when he tried to mount his horse. Instead, Colt led him toward Daniel Yost's mercantile store.

As they walked down the boardwalk, Chris said, "You know Yost?"

"Yes."

"I need you to keep him occupied in his store," Colt said. "He has a big collection of tack for horses and knows a lot about it. Get him in a discussion about snaffle bits and curb bits and ask which is better and all. Just keep him in the store."

"Where will you be?" Man Killer asked.

"Climbing up into his office upstairs," Colt said. "I got some suspicions and want a quick look at his books."

Man Killer spoke to the man for ten minutes about what kind of bit he should use for breaking horses and actually ordered several snaffle bits, since Yost convinced him that they were less severe than curb bits for the job.

Man killer quit talking when he saw Colt pass by on his way to the horses.

Mounting up outside, Man Killer said, "Did you find what you want?"

"Maybe," Colt said with no further explanation.

The mysterious answer didn't bother the Nez Perce. He knew Colt would explain when the time was right.

A short while later, they rode up to Man Killer's ranch, and his wife, Jennifer Banta, wrapped her arms around her husband, giving him a passionate kiss. Then, she saw the look on his face.

Jennifer forced a smile and said, "Chris Colt is going off on some dangerous mission, and you're going with him, right?"

He hesitated a second and replied, "Yes."

Colt chuckled nervously.

She tried hard to suppress a smile and said, "Let's go inside and pack you some food and provisions."

He kissed her, and they all walked inside together.

Jennifer Banta accepted scenes like this when she married Man Killer. She would rather try to rope a cyclone than force him to stay away from a situation where he felt he could make a major contribution, even if it meant him being in grave danger to do it.

Colt was ready to leave when Man Killer

came out, but he dropped off his horse and walked up to Jennifer and gave her a big hug.

Colt whispered, "Thanks for sharing him. I'll keep an eye on him."

She slapped his arm and said, "Who's going to keep an eye on you?"

Man Killer chuckled, saying, "Mandy."

Embarrassed, Colt tossed an apple at Man Killer, hitting him squarely in the ribs. The Nez Perce winced while he laughed.

Jennifer said, "What? Who?"

"He just made that up," Colt responded.

Feeling it was a good time to change the subject, Man Killer grinned at his friend, saying, "I am ready to go, Great Tracker."

Colt smiled, and mounted his horse, waving to Jennifer. He squeezed War Bonnet's ribs with his calves and the horse started away, with Man Killer riding next to him.

The two men headed on south toward Alamosa, where they could board a freight to Durango. From Durango, they would detour north to Silverton to get information about the gang and their activities.

There was a giant desolate Navajo reservation that covered millions of square miles in the three territories, and the bad men were hiding there somewhere. It would be Colt and Man

Killer's challenge to find them, and safely rescue Chris's sister in the process.

Their first stop would be the sheriff's office in Durango. They arrived after many hours of hard travel, so they put the horses up for a rest in a livery stable and got a pair of nice rooms at the Strater Hotel, the finest hotel in downtown Durango. They decided to take the train that ran the narrow valley up to Silverton in the morning, get their questions answered there and ride back, leaving their horses in the livery stable.

The sheriff was gone for the night, so the pair went to a saloon they had not been to before in Durango, not far from the Strater. The saloon was wild and raucous, filled with miners, a few railroad men, and several cowboys.

Chris and Man Killer walked up to the bar and ordered two beers. The bartender never even looked up at them. He simply drew one beer from the tap and placed it in front of Colt, then turned away wiping glasses.

Colt said, "Excuse me, sir. We ordered two beers."

The bartender didn't even turn around, saying, "Sorry, don't serve redskins."

Colt gritted his teeth and said, "This is Man Killer. He used to be a deputy U.S. marshal. He has done more to clean up this territory than any ten white men."

The bartender, a very large man with fists the size of hams, turned around, grinning. He glanced at Man Killer, then back at Colt. His glare was challenging.

"Did you say *used* to be deputy marshal?"

"Yep," Colt said.

The bartender said, "Then I guess *now* he ain't nothin' more than any other blanket nigger."

Colt balled his hand into a fist, and Man Killer's hand shot out and caught his arm.

"Let's drink somewhere else, my brother," Man Killer said softly.

The bartender blew on a glass, saying, "Sounds like a right good idea to me."

Colt looked at a smaller man heading out the door, saying, "Get the deputy marshal and tell him to come here."

The man, wide-eyed, nodded and headed out the door.

Colt and Man Killer stood there while several of the bartender's buddies, well into their cups, spread out around the two in strategic positions for a fight. Chris and Man Killer gave each other knowing looks, almost able to read each other's minds in such a situation.

A few tense minutes passed, and another

large man, this one covered with freckles and baby fat, walked through the door. He was wearing a badge.

"Are you the deputy marshal?" Chris asked.

"Aye, that I am, sir. What seems to be the ruckus?"

"This barkeep refused to serve my friend a drink because he is an Indian," Colt said.

"Who might you be, sir?"

"Colt, Chris Colt."

There was a murmur around the room.

The deputy said, "Aye, I thought you looked familiar. No matter. His saloon, he don't have ta serve red niggers Marshal . . . I mean Mr. Colt."

"Yes, he does. This man has civil rights," Colt said.

"Fine," the marshal said, "then sue him, but I'm not making anybody serve no drink to a red nigger."

Chris Colt sighed.

"Let's leave," Man Killer said.

"No," Colt said firmly.

Man Killer knew the subject was closed. They were in for some kind of fight. He wondered how Colt was going to handle this situation. What Man Killer did not know was that Chris Colt wondered himself how he was going to do it.

Colt walked over to the marshal, whose hand went down and rested on his gun handle.

Colt put his arm around the deputy's big beefy shoulder and said quietly, "Let's go outside and talk for a minute. Shall we?"

The two walked outside, and once on the wooden sidewalk outside the large saloon batwing doors, Colt stepped back and lit a cigar. He offered one to the deputy and lit it for him.

Colt blew a puff skyward thoughtfully then looked the deputy in the eye.

"Let's get right to it. I was a Deputy U.S. Marshal, and so was my friend, who is like a brother to me. He has scars all over his body from risking his life saving the likes of you and that idiot in the saloon. Because I have respect for the law, I invited you out here to speak privately, instead of embarrassing you in there in front of those men. Now, both the bartender, and you yourself insulted my friend by calling him a nasty name in there. I have one question, Deputy: What did Man Killer or I ever do to you to cause you to treat us with such disrespect?"

The deputy was flustered and thought for a minute, and Colt kept perfectly quiet waiting for an answer.

The lawman finally said, "Well, nothin.' I never met either one a ya before."

"Then good," Colt said. "You won't mind walking back inside with me and apologizing to my friend for what you called him. You can do it quietly so you won't get embarrassed, then you can leave and go make your rounds. I'll straighten out our little problem with the barkeep."

The deputy now hitched up his pants and threw his shoulders back, saying, "See here. You trying to tell me what to do?"

Colt stared in his eyes and said, "Yes."

Colt didn't blink. The deputy did.

Finally, he said, "Aye, that doesn't really sound unreasonable, I guess."

The two walked back into the saloon and the deputy walked over to Man Killer with Colt right behind him.

The deputy leaned over and said very quietly, "I apologize for calling you a red nigger."

Man Killer nodded and the red-faced deputy turned and walked out the door.

Colt turned toward the bartender as one of the saloon-rats, his crossed guns hanging low, approached him. There was menace in his eyes and whiskey on his breath. He approached Colt and looked into his eyes.

"You keep away from my pardner here," he said.

Colt said, "Move your hands from the guns, friend. That could get a man killed."

The little guy sneered, "You think I'm scared of you, Colt?"

"I could care less," Chris said. "Just move your hands away from the gun butts slowly."

Colt kept inching closer as he talked.

The man's cheek quivered as he said, "You know how many hours a day I practice my quick draw?"

"How many of those cans you've shot at ever shot back? Now, move your hands away for the last time," Colt demanded.

The man gave it away in his eyes first, which was always the way. As soon as Colt saw the man give a quick blink, he went into action. His hands shot out just as the man's hand closed on the crossed pistols. Colt pushed the man's wrist against his body, and yanked upward. Both pistols flew out of the man's hands and into the air. Colt caught both and cocked them, sticking them up against the man's chest. In a show of gun handling, he then uncocked them, spun them forward, then backward, did a border shift, spun them backward and stopped them, hurled them around butts out, then quickly back in, and then neatly shoved them back into the would-be shootist's holsters. There was a low whistle in the back of the room.

Colt stared at the ashen-faced little man, saying, "You still here?"

The man almost ran from the saloon.

Colt turned to the bartender and smiled. "My friend wants a beer."

The bartender, a hardcase wanting to show off, said, "You don't scare me none, Colt. What are you going to do, shoot an unarmed man?"

"No," Colt replied.

With that, Colt's hand shot out across the bar and grabbed the bartender by the lapels. Chris pulled the two-hundred-and-fifty-pounder across the bar with no more effort than pulling a canoe out of the water. He kept pulling until the man's feet dropped off the bar and onto the floor. Then Chris, still gripping the man's lapels with one hand, slapped him across the face five times in rapid succession.

Colt jerked the man up until their faces almost met and gritted his teeth, saying, "You want to show off for your friends some more? Well, show off. Come on, show off."

Colt repeated his lightning-fast staccato slapping assault and said, "Come on!"

The bartender's face was beet red from the slaps and one nostril started bleeding.

He worked up his nerve and drew back a beefy fist, but Colt had been waiting for just that move. Colt shoved him backward, and the small of the man's back slammed against the edge of the bar, the wind leaving him in a rush. His eyes flashed in panic as he tried to catch his breath, and Colt hit him in the stomach with a vicious right hand. After he recovered from the blow, he started to vomit and ran outside, his hand over his mouth. Chris leaned against the bar, waiting for the man to return. He staggered back inside after a few minutes, and slowly made it back behind the bar.

Colt leaned against the bar, now saying in a friendly voice, "My friend would like a cold beer."

The man meekly poured a draft for Man Killer and placed it in front of him. Man Killer nodded and smiled, offering the glass up in toast to the bartender. "Thank you."

After Man Killer drank, the two men walked out of the saloon without anyone saying a word.

The next morning, they stopped at the sheriff's office and spoke to a deputy, as the sheriff was out of town. They learned that the gang rode to Silverton and horribly injured two prostitutes, but what happened near Durango was worse.

The deputy sheriff was named Harley Roberts, and he was from south Texas.

He said, "Wal, these four yahoos rode up ta the Cannister ranch. It's a little cow spread over on the west part a the county and was owned by one of our deputy sheriffs. We're kinda spread out, and he handled that part of the county pretty much. Mrs. Cannister, she was a real looker, and when they got there we figure she was home alone. Wal, you don't want to hear how they done her. Then the sign looks like the husband, two sons, and the daughter come ridin' up in a wagon. It was full a fencin' tools, so's they mus' a all been out ta mend fence. It looks like mebbe they shot the pa from ambush along with one boy, and then tied up them two and the other one, and made 'em watch whilst they done the daughter up like they done the ma. Then they shot 'em to doll rags with a durned Gatling gun. Them Cannister boys must a had twenty bullet holes apiece in 'em. And them two womenfolk—I never seen the like."

"They're holed up in Four Corners?" Man Killer asked.

"Near as I know," the deputy replied, "but they got a bunch a posses down there along with the sheriff, and some Pinkertons, and the army, but they're all fightin' each other more than the owlhoots."

Colt shook his head. They thanked the deputy and headed for the train. They rode the scenic valley up to Silverton and were immediately guided to the doctor's office and clinic where one prostitute was recovering from wounds. They looked at her and winced. She looked like someone who once had a pretty face, even with a bunch of makeup on it. Unfortunately, her eyes were swollen shut, her lips swollen, nose smashed, and it looked like she was cut all over her face by a razor or sharp knife. She was still out cold, so they were taken to the brothel where the other prostitute lived and worked.

The madam came down the winding staircase of the two-story frame house. She was wearing a frilly bright red dress, and her eyes lit up when she saw Colt and Man Killer.

"Well, aren't you two strapping big men," she cooed. "What kind of girls are you looking for? We can help you out."

Colt removed his hat, and her face flushed.

"Ma'am, we want to speak with the young lady that was attacked."

The woman made a face, saying, "Are you lawmen?"

"No ma'am, but we aim to find the men that attacked them," Colt said.

"Sir, that is fine, but Brandy is pretty hurt and shaken still. How do you know you will get them?"

Man Killer said, "Because the mighty Colt has gotten every bad man he has gone after."

Her eyes really lit up. "Are you Chris Colt?" she asked.

Colt nodded.

"My word. Then you must be Man Killer. Boys, this is indeed a pleasure. Speaking of which, you can have anybody in the house, including me. What is your pleasure?"

"No offense, ma'am, but my wife is my pleasure," Man Killer said.

"No wonder you two are such heroes. How about you, Mr. Colt?"

He smiled, saying, "Call me Chris, please. And my only pleasure would be to interview Brandy."

"Of course, darling, anything you want," she said.

She took them upstairs to a room at the end of a long hall. A very pretty woman lay in a large feather bed with posters on each corner and a large canopy over it. Her full head of beautiful auburn hair reminded Colt of his late wife. She was ravishing, even with the cut cheekbone and black eye.

Brandy had an angry look on her face, saying, "Cookie, I told you I can't work yet. These—"

The madam cut her off saying, "Relax, honey. This here's the famous Chris Colt and Man Killer. They just want to talk with you. They want to get the men who did this to you."

Brandy sat up and grabbed her ribs in pain. She patted the bed, and both men sat down on either side of her.

She smiled, looking at both of them, saying, "I wish I *was* working right now."

Colt smiled.

The madam said, "Are you kidding, honey? I asked them what their pleasure was, and Man Killer here said it was his wife."

"If we would have met men like these before, we never would have gotten into this profession," Brandy said.

"Brandy, what can you tell us about these men?" Colt asked.

"Easy. They're poison, rattlesnake mean. I got this," she said, indicating her eye and cheek, "and broken ribs, but you should see the other girl."

"We did," Man Killer said.

"All four of them were white. Three of them

were with me, and one was with Sarah. He carried a straight razor and used it on her. He was the only small one. But he is their leader. Ready to draw his pistol at any time. His name was Buzztail, and he acted like one. The other three were all big, real big. I mean, even taller than you, Mr. Colt."

"Chris."

"They were much taller than you, and big around the bodies. None of them was under three hundred pounds, but Buzztail couldn't have been too much bigger than me," she said.

She stopped for water and held her ribs. Chris poured her some more, and she said, "Thanks, Mr. Colt."

She rested a minute and went on. "Sometimes, we'll get men in here who rough us up. That is one of the hazards of our jobs, but there aren't too many like that. If a gang of rough ones comes in, maybe sometimes one will beat on us, but all four of these men were mean. Low down mean."

She thought for a minute and added, "I think they might have been soldiers, too."

"Why?" Man Killer asked.

She replied, "The other three kept calling Buzztail, sir, and I had a feeling that Buzztail was not a nickname. You know, like it was a code name, or something like spies would use."

She had to stop for a few minutes as her ribs really started hurting. She fell back on the pillow and started crying. Sweat broke out on her face, and Chris Colt dampened a washcloth and carefully swabbed her forehead. She opened her eyes, smiling up at him.

"Where were you a few years ago, big man?" Brandy sighed.

"With my wife," Colt said.

She said, "Yes, I heard about that. I'm sorry. But I'll tell you what. I'd go through the pain tonight just to have you stay here and not think about her for one night. No charge."

Colt smiled, saying, "Ma'am, thank you, I guess, but nothing would ever make me forget about my wife. Is there anything else you could think of?"

She sat up again, moaning as she did.

"They talked about the Big Gun," she said. "Later I heard they had a Gatling. They also spoke about a robbery or something."

"How's that?" Colt asked.

She said, "They referred to it differently. You know, that's why I said I thought they were Army. I know. They kept calling it the operation, not the job or the hold-up, or other things I've heard men call a robbery, but the operation."

"Anything else?" Chris asked.

"Yes," she said. "Another gang showed up and met them. They had a gorgeous blond woman with them, and she was their prisoner. Her hands were tied."

"My sister," Colt said.

"No!" Brandy cried out. "No wonder. One of them kept talking about a large ransom."

"The ones who held my sister, were any of them Indians?"

She shook her head and thought for a minute to try to remember anything else. Colt stood up, and Man Killer followed suit. Chris reached into his pocket and pulled out five twenty-dollar gold pieces.

He placed them in her hand, and she shook her head, tears in her eyes.

Colt smiled softly, saying, "You're a little stove up right now, ma'am, but in your job, you get paid for your time. And I insist on paying you for your time."

"Bless you, gentlemen," she said.

The two men walked out of the room, and thanked the madam at the door before boarding the train back to Durango.

Riding the train, Colt spoke to Man Killer. "What do you think?"

Man Killer grinned, saying, "I think we should go back and get that Brandy and one of her friends, a few bottles of champagne, and leave for New Orleans or maybe France. What do you think? Good idea? Charley will get herself out of trouble."

Colt started laughing and punched Man Killer on the upper arm. Man Killer fell over sideways holding his biceps and laughing. Colt, laughed again, and punched Man Killer in the thigh. The conductor walked by giving them both a funny look. After laughing and giggling like a couple of schoolboys, relieving their own fears and tension, the two men got more serious.

"They are probably soldiers who deserted," Man Killer said. "That way they would know where to steal a Gatling gun, and how to use it."

"What do you suppose the operation could be?" Colt asked.

"I don't know. How about you? What do you think?"

"Well, we have to figure out what would make them bring a Gatling gun this direction and where they were heading. What would be the target?"

"Maybe they want to hold up a big bank," Man Killer said.

"Maybe, but why would they need a Gatling gun? A cannon to get into a vault, maybe, but not a Gatling gun," Colt said. "I don't think so. A bank just doesn't make sense."

"Then what else could be their target?" Man Killer asked.

"It would have to be one that would need more firepower to whip," Colt said. "A Gatling gun gives you bullets fast, and lots of them."

"A stagecoach with a lot of money?" Man Killer offered.

"Maybe, but hardcases like these would simply rob a stage. They wouldn't have to have a Gatling gun," Colt said.

The two men talked about the possibilities while they rode to the Cannister ranch. At the ranch, they searched for any possible additional clues but found none. The two men headed on toward Four Corners. They would camp east of Cortez, then head down toward the San Juan in Utah from there.

They still had not reached the river by the next afternoon, so they camped near a place called Cross Canyon. Colt and Man Killer were used to trees and green grass, at least in clumps, but here they were seeing dry sage and rocks.

And sand—lots of it. The weather here, just a few hours away from the cooler climate of the mountains, was desert hot.

Where the two men dropped down into Cross Canyon, they could see nothing but cliffs on both sides and a big wide gulch opening up to Montezuma Creek, which poured into the San Juan River. That was the area where the killers were supposed to be hiding. Leaving the Hovenweep area, the two trackers headed west, riding slowly in the burning sun.

Looking at the sheer cliffs and rocky overhangs, and feeling the searing heat, Man Killer reflected back to his first meeting with Geronimo at his rancheria. Man Killer had shot it out with three of Geronimo's men and had killed two but only wounded the third. It was in the deserts of Arizona, not too far from where he and Colt were now and the terrain and climate were very similar. He remembered his meeting with Lozen, who became quite famous as a female warrior fighting alongside Geronimo. He was in love with and engaged to Jennifer at the time, but had carried the wounded Apache through the desert heat, and was taken to Geronimo's rancheria after fainting. He had quite a surprise when he awoke.

* * *

Man Killer struggled through the veil of blackness and realized he had long been unconscious. It was not a strong realization, but rather a slow, growing awareness. He started recognizing smells—burning mesquite, pine needles, leather, corn, sweet bread, the scent of a woman. His eyes wanted to open, but he felt himself slipping back into blackness again. He wanted to see Jennifer again, however, so he decided to leave the comfortable blackness and force his eyes open. He looked up into a pair of black eyes. His head was on the lap of an Apache warrior. No, he thought, it was an Apache woman. Then he saw that it was an Apache woman dressed like a warrior. Her eyes were smiling as she gave him some more water.

"You have been a long time in the land of many dreams, Pierced Nose," she said. "How are you called?"

He said, "I am Man Killer of the Nez Perce. Who are you?"

"I am called Lozen."

Man Killer sat up suddenly and his head swam. "Lozen, the famous warrior woman who fights with Geronimo?"

"You know of my name?" she replied, genuinely surprised.

"All who follow the trail of words about the

Apache know of Lozen, the warrior woman," he said.

"This is true?"

Man Killer replied, "This is true. Where am I?"

He did not thank her for his care, as that was not the Indian way. Gratitude was always understood.

Lozen replied, "The rancheria of Geronimo."

Man Killer was surprised, saying, "Why do I live?"

"No one questions Geronimo. He is wise."

As if it were a given signal, none other than Geronimo himself entered the wickiup and looked down at Man Killer.

Man Killer said, "You are Geronimo, a mighty enemy and great leader. I am Man Killer of the Nez Perce."

"And you were a scout who led the buffalo soldiers against Victorio and his people," Geronimo said.

Man Killer smiled and said, "Victorio was a great warrior and hard to defeat."

"You are the brother to the great scout called Colt?" Geronimo asked.

"I am proud to be the brother of Wamble Uncha as the Lakotah call him. I live in his lodges, and we ride on the same lands side by side," Man Killer said.

"He is not here now," Geronimo said.

Man Killer replied, "He is at his lodge with his woman and children. He has two children now, a son and a daughter."

"You scout for Al Seiber?"

"Yes," Man Killer said.

Geronimo grinned and said, "They send you alone after my warriors because you are not Apache or Navajo."

Man Killer smiled. "Why am I not walking the spirit trail now, Geronimo?"

Geronimo said, "It was not your time. You carried Strong Rope on your shoulders and cared for his wounds. Why did you not kill him and go?"

Man Killer said, "I do not make war on men who cannot fight back, or on women, or children."

He glanced over at Lozen and added, "Except maybe some women who fight as good as any man."

"How many wives do you have?" Lozen asked.

"I have none," Man Killer replied.

Boldly, Lozen said to Geronimo, "This one could make me work among the wickiups with the other women and make babies."

Man Killer blushed a deep red, and Geronimo left the wickiup, grinning.

No sooner did Geronimo leave than Lozen stared into Man Killer's eyes and quickly removed her clothing, standing before him totally naked.

Man Killer looked away and said, "Lozen could only be the woman of a mighty shaman like Geronimo."

She moved down to him and dropped upon her knees directly in front of him. Her hand went up under the tanned antelope hide covering his own nakedness. His breath caught, and he looked away from her, not speaking.

"Or the mighty warrior Man Killer. Why do you not look upon the body of Lozen? Do you not want to lay with me?"

Man Killer gulped and said, "Yes, very much."

He sat up with a look like an excited little boy, continuing, "But, Lozen, my heart is with another woman. When my thoughts are of her, my heart sings."

Lozen was angry. "She is of the Pierced Nose?" she snapped.

"No, she is of the white-eyes," Man Killer said.

Lozen spat at him and stormed out of the wickiup, her clothes in her hand. He struggled to his feet and then to the door, watching the naked woman warrior as she stormed past several men. One pointed at her and held his bow, making some phallic joke with it to two others who laughed. She stopped, picked up a rock, and slugged the brave squarely in the face with it, sending him reeling over a bush onto his back. The others laughed at him while she walked into the brush.

Man Killer went back to the fur bed and lay down, his head spinning. He drank several gourds full of water from an earthen pot and felt a little better. His eyes closed, and he fell asleep instantly. His dreams were of a beautiful blond maiden, green grass, and high mountain lakes.

"Man Killer, Man Killer!" Colt snapped.

Man Killer snapped out of his daydream and looked at Colt.

"Thinking about Jennifer?" Colt asked.

This embarrassed Man Killer, as he was actually thinking about another woman.

"No, I was remembering my capture by Geronimo."

Colt chuckled, saying, "In other words, you were daydreaming about Lozen. This landscape sure reminds me of that country. Make sure while you daydream that you pay attention to possible ambush sites."

Man Killer nodded and scanned the canyon walls to his right. Within minutes, he was thinking again about his capture.

Lozen rode out from the rancheria and thought of killing more white-eyes and Mexicans. She usually kept more to herself and had been photographed by the white-eyes only one time, while many in Geronimo's band had had their pictures made many times. From then on, she decided, she would not again make her feelings known to another man. She would show them how a woman could fight.

That had been along time ago, Man Killer remembered, but this land and this heat made it seem as though it had just been a few days. He looked over at Colt to see if he could tell if the tracker looked any older, but Man Killer could not see any noticeable difference.

Then he remembered Colt, telling him, "Only the mountains don't change, people do."

Man Killer again thought back to the adventure in the camp of Geronimo.

*   *   *

At the end of the second day of resting, Geronimo entered the wickiup of Man Killer and beckoned, "Come."

Man Killer, feeling much better and stronger now, followed the legendary Apache across the rancheria. They came to another wickiup at the end of the village and Geronimo showed the scout the way in. The shaman left, and Man Killer entered. Inside, Strong Rope sat up and looked at the Nez Perce. He stuck out his hand, and the two shook, holding on to each other's forearms. They spoke for several hours, and Man Killer came to respect the young warrior.

He was surprised to find out that people were pretty much the same all over. Living among the whites, he had seen it, just as he had in the lodges of the Nez Perce. There were those who were brave and those who were not; those who were strong, and those who were weak; some who spoke much, and those who spoke little. Chief Joseph spoke seldom but very seriously and eloquently when he did. Joseph's brother, Ollikut, however, talked incessantly and was a great joker, clowning around with everyone.

It was the next day that Man Killer approached Geronimo about leaving.

The Apache said, "You cannot leave."

"Why not?" Man Killer asked.

Geronimo said, "I should kill you. Will you not scout against us for the bluecoats?"

"It is my job," Man Killer replied.

"It is my job to stop you," Geronimo said.

The scout said, "I cannot stay."

"If you leave, you must die," Geronimo said.

"When I can, I will go," Man Killer said.

The Apache responded, "Then you will soon walk the spirit trail with those who have defied Geronimo."

"I was not given my name because I pick flowers," Man Killer said.

"Maybe I will kill you now," Geronimo said.

"No, you will not," Man Killer replied.

"Why will I not?"

"Because that is not Geronimo's way," the Nez Perce said. "You will wait to see if I leave, then try to kill me."

"And so it shall be, young brother. My heart will be heavy when I steal your spirit. The wind is now blowing. What comes with it?"

"Geronimo!" An Apache ran up, yelling, "Juh and others come with a white-eyes—a captive."

Man Killer snapped out of his daydream again and looked over at Colt.

The Nez Perce started to speak when Colt surprised him saying, "Still thinking about that time when you were a captive of Geronimo, weren't you?"

Man Killer grinned, saying, "You do the right work. You can even track my thoughts as they move across my mind."

"It's pretty easy. I was thinking back on that time, too. This terrain and the heat reminds me of it all."

As they rode on, both thought back to what happened at the camp when the announcement was made to Geronimo that a prisoner was being brought in. The images were still very clear in Man Killer's mind.

Geronimo watched as the small party rounded the trail along the steep cliffside and walked through the trees into the rancheria. Man Killer grinned as he saw Chris Colt riding in, waving and nodding at Geronimo.

What also excited Man Killer was the sight of Hawk, his horse, being led by one of the Apaches. Chris Colt, atop War Bonnet, was being led by a rawhide-braided rope around his neck. He was still grinning and nodding at Apaches right and left as he was brought toward Geronimo.

Smiling broadly, Colt winked at one ugly woman and said, "Morning, ma'am."

Looking at her husband, who did not understand English either, he said, "Howdy, sir, if we get into a fight, I'm going to let you live. That will fix you."

They pulled up in front of Naiche, who had been Geronimo's right-hand warrior, and a legendary shaman in his own right.

Geronimo simply said, "Colt."

Chris nodded at the Apache shaman, and said, "Naiche, howdy. Geronimo, it's been a long time, you old throat-slitter. I came here in peace to parley. Your boys here don't understand it. I left my guns in my saddlebags and put the sneak on them at their cooking fire. I walked up and grabbed a piece of rabbit and started eating it. Finally, after seeing me, these brave warriors held guns on me, tied my wrists, and brought me here. Mighty brave Chirichajua you got here." Colt gave a little chuckle.

Geronimo looked at Juh, who looked down at his hands.

The Apache leader then said, "Untie him. Give him his weapons."

Colt held his hands back while another warrior cut through the bonds with a razor-sharp knife. He removed the noose and swung his left leg over the neck of the big paint and slid out of the saddle, landing in front of Geronimo. He stuck his hand out and the two clasped forearms.

Colt then looked at Man Killer and said, "So, you got sick of white people and decided to join up with Geronimo, huh?"

"Yes, Geronimo has been telling me to leave, and I have been begging him to let me stay," Man Killer said.

"Colt," Geronimo said, "you have come far. Tonight you will sleep in the wickiup of your Pierced-Nose brother, and we will talk when the sun starts his walk across the sky again."

Chris Colt nodded and tossed Geronimo a small oilskin sack, explaining, "Coffee and sugar for your fire tonight."

Geronimo turned and walked away.

Chris and Man Killer ate antelope stew, talking and smoking long into the night.

The next morning, Geronimo came to the wickiup and said simply, "Let us three walk together and talk."

They walked away from the rancheria and sat on rocks overlooking a steep thousand foot cliff, the Sierra Madre range far below running south into Mexico.

Colt pulled out three cigars and lit one for each man. They blew smoke to the four compass points, and Geronimo offered a silent prayer, then they each enjoyed the cigars and talked.

"You have come for your young brother?" Geronimo asked.

"I have."

"I cannot let him leave."

"You are Geronimo." Colt laughed, and continued, "Most folks would say you can do anything you want."

Geronimo puffed his chest out a little and looked out over the mountains, saying, "Tell me, Colt. You were respected by Cochise, even back when we first met. Do you think the white-eyes will treat my people right if I surrender?"

"Probably not."

"You are more like Apache than white," Geronimo said.

"There are honorable white men, Geronimo," Colt said.

"Some," Geronimo said, "but I cannot let your friend leave. He leads the Long Knives against us. We are enemies."

"You and I are enemies, but we respect each other," Colt replied. "Geronimo, what if I give you my word that he will not scout against you?"

"Then he can leave."

"I cannot give my word. I was hired to do a job," Man Killer said.

"But I am a chief of scouts," Colt said, "and you only work when I say so. You are fired."

Man Killer grinned.

Geronimo said, "You may go, but first I must have your word that you will not make war against me or my people, Colt."

"Unless my family is attacked by your people," Colt responded.

"That will not happen," Geronimo promised.

They left the cliffside and returned to the rancheria.

On the way, Geronimo said, "You know the location of my rancheria."

Man Killer replied, "So we do, but Colt's word has been given. We do not twist words when speaking from the heart." Saying this, he touched his breast.

"Another Colt with red skin, this one is. He killed three of my warriors. He wounded the best, treated the man's wounds, and carried him on his shoulders, looking for water," Geronimo said.

Colt grinned and said, "I would have slit your warrior's throat and left him there."

Geronimo gave out a howl and said, "So would Geronimo." They took a few more steps and Geronimo added, "Perhaps Man Killer has stronger shoulders than us, old warrior."

Colt smiled, looking off at the horizon, and thinking of the real meaning of the wise leader's words.

"Perhaps," he replied.

At the rancheria, Man Killer was given his weapons, and he went straightaway to Hawk and petted him all over.

Geronimo watched this while sharing another cigar with Colt, and said, "He is a strange one, this warrior."

"No, his ways are just different from yours," Colt replied. "He is of a different nation and has also lived among the whites a long time now."

Colt then handed Geronimo a leather parfleche and said, "A gift for my enemy."

"I must give you a gift, too," Geronimo said.

Colt looked at Man Killer and back at the Apache, winking, saying, "You already have."

Both men were thinking of that day still as they rode slowly along, their mouths getting so dry and free of spittle that their tongues were actually feeling as though they were made of dry leaves.

Man Killer teased, "Do you remember your big fight with that big mean woman?"

Colt grinned. "She was tough!"

They both thought back to the incident after Geronimo had given his permission for them to leave.

Man Killer mounted up and walked his horse over to Colt. He started to say something to Geronimo, but was interrupted by the sight of Lozen, her jaw firmly thrust forward, striding up to them.

"He cannot leave," she said.

"Why?" Geronimo asked.

"I challenge him to a fight to the death."

Man Killer raised his eyebrows and whispered to Colt. "Lozen is mad because I won't be her stallion."

"She probably has her pick of stallions. She is mad because you won't be her mate," Colt said.

The gauntlet had been thrown down, and Geronimo would not let them leave without accepting the challenge. Both scouts knew this.

Man Killer and Colt dismounted, and Man Killer said, "Lozen, you do not want to do this thing."

Lozen spoke between clenched teeth, her lips curled back. "Yes, I do." She drew her knife and started circling him in a crouched position.

Man Killer crossed his arms over his chest,

standing tall, and said, "I do not make war on women."

"Friend, you better, or she's going to run you through with that pig-sticker," Colt said.

Man Killer stood there firmly, arms crossed.

"Fight or die!" Lozen spat.

She started to lunge forward and Colt stepped forward with his hand up, saying, "Wait, hold up. Geronimo, he will not fight her, but I will. Is that okay?"

Geronimo looked at Lozen, so mad now she just wanted to stab anybody, so she nodded her head affirmatively.

Colt pulled Man Killer out of the way and whispered, "Stay with the horses."

"No, this is my fight," Man Killer said.

Gritting his teeth, Colt said, "But you aren't fighting."

Man Killer kept quiet when he saw the look on Chris's face, knowing that Colt meant he was not to be argued with.

Colt said again, "I will fight you, Lozen."

She came forward and slashed with the knife. As her hand went across his body with the blade, he pulled his midsection back, and the blade just passed by it.

Colt looked down quickly and pointed at her right foot, saying, "Your foot's bleeding."

She looked down quickly, and Chris launched a right uppercut from the hip that literally made her body arch backward through the air. Colt stepped forward and pulled the knife from her still fingers. She did not move.

"Kill her," Geronimo said. "It is your right."

Colt tossed the knife to the Apache and said, "Nope, I was trying to prevent a killing. I don't make war on women either. Something to think about, old enemy," Colt added. "No matter how many whites and Mexicans you kill, it won't bring your wife and daughters back. And doing what the Mexicans did to them doesn't make you any better than them, does it?"

"Maybe this is true," Geronimo said. "I will think on it."

He raised his hand and waved.

Looking up at the cliff walls of Cross Canyon, the two trackers now seemed higher, the canyon larger. Chris said, "Let's camp on Montezuma Creek today and head on down to the San Juan after dark, or get up real early while it's still somewhat cool out."

"That is a very good idea," Man Killer said. "The horses are very hot already, and so am I."

"The sand on the floor of the canyon and the really hard rocks around here that don't absorb anything but reflect the heat, it just makes riding through here like riding around inside a Dutch oven," Colt said.

A coyote stopped in mid-stride. He turned his head and his ears perked up, twisting left and right. It was instinctive for him to not stand still very long. His head rose slightly and his little nostrils started flaring as he tested the wind. The hot, dry, acrid heat was like the inside of Satan's oven loaded with coals and brimstone, but to the coyote, it was something only mildly uncomfortable that made his tongue loll out and pant heavily.

There was movement, and he spotted a scorpion moving across the desert sand. His attention went back to sniffing the wind.

Suddenly, it shifted again, and he waited. The smell would return. His mind instinctively catalogued the various smells wafting through his nostrils. Cacti, old urine from a desert bighorn sheep, very faint odors from a decaying mule, a deer carcass five miles distant, blood, feces, death, gun oil, vomit, gunpowder, leather, steel, horses, buzzards, and humans. These were all dangerous smells, and he wanted to run, but the scents of blood, urine, feces, and death attracted him, so he would move closer, following the smell, his senses even keener, more alert.

He would travel fast, but only a few feet at a time, his eyes, ears, and nose checking all about him with each halt to ensure there was no enemy nearby. The coyote bitch was one-quarter mile out to the south, but her eyes had been on him, and she knew he had a scent. The two always hunted in pairs and had greater success that way, sometimes one jumping a quarry that would run in abject fear, circling back close to the other mate, who would pick up the chase while the first one rested. Jackrabbits and kangaroo rats aside, these hunters, however, preferred finding carrion when it was available. Even though the man-smell signaled danger, they had eaten that meat once before, and it sated their appetites. He smelled vulture, so there was carrion there where the smells were originating from. The coyote soon walked up to an old Navajo lying facedown on the floor of Cross Canyon. The sheepherder had made the mistake of running into the killers along the San Juan River. Chock full of bullet holes, he had tried to walk all the way back home to the Hovenweep area but only made it this far before dying.

The coyote moved around the dead body, but then the fresh man-smell got even stronger.

Then he saw the two men approaching from the canyon on their big horses. He gave a low growl that the men could not possibly hear. Then he paced back and forth behind this free dinner, and finally, begrudgingly gave up the meal and wandered off down the canyon.

Chris spotted the body first and immediately drew his Peacemaker. He clucked with his tongue, and Man Killer drew his gun before he even looked over at Colt.

They circled around the body, looking at every conceivable hiding spot for bushwhackers. Finally, they rode up to the corpse and both men dismounted. Rolling him over, they saw the bullet holes all over his chest and stomach. Chris looked up at Man Killer, and they both shook their heads simultaneously.

Man Killer finally broke the silence. "They shot him to have fun."

"Some fun," Colt said.

Man Killer nodded sadly.

"I think we should take the time to try to find his home and take his body," Chris said. "I'll head up the gulch and see if I can spot some old tracks of his heading down."

Colt returned ten minutes later.

"He was a sheepherder," he said. "He took a

flock down and apparently got shot while he was with them."

"He was probably at the river when he was shot," Man Killer said. "I bet you he took the animals to stay beside the river, because it is so dry here. I bet you that even Montezuma Creek gets dried up sometimes when it gets hotter."

"Don't even tell me that it is going to get hotter," Colt said.

They packed up the body and took it home to his family, which was five miles distant. He was indeed a sheepherder and left behind a wife and five children. The family seemed grateful but were also somewhat distant. Colt and Man Killer were offered food for their trouble and ate a meal of tortillas along with Navajo fry bread, which Colt developed an immediate taste for.

After that, they refused the opportunity to stay for the night and headed back down to Cross Canyon. They were told by the oldest son that the killers were hiding along the river in old Anasazi ruins.

The Anasazi were the "people who came before." They were cliff dwellers, making their homes along the many rocky cliff faces in the area, sometimes locating entire complexes on cliffs with very large overhangs.

They made camp and started talking about

the possibilities again. It was puzzling to both of them, very puzzling, indeed.

Man Killer said, "We have thought of several things that these men might have stolen the gun for, correct?"

"That's right," Colt replied.

"Everything we have thought about has always been related to money, so far."

"Isn't that why most people steal, lie, and cheat?" Colt asked.

"You said most people, not all people."

Chris chewed on a leaf of peppermint from his saddlebag. He grinned broadly. "Good point, Man Killer," he said. "We have been limiting ourselves in what we are thinking about."

"What else could they be after?" Man Killer asked.

"Let's banty that around a bit," Colt said.

The two men talked for another hour about the possibilities, but came to no conclusion. They slept and awoke in the middle of the night. Colt built a fire of dried wood, which was plentiful in the arid canyon.

Over breakfast, Man Killer, who was very well read, suddenly thought of something and was very excited.

"Have you ever heard of the Navajo Curse?" he queried.

"No. What is it?"

Man Killer then related the story about the so-called curse of the Navajo tribe. It concerned the area they were now in.

In the year of 1776, there was a Spanish exploration party in the region, headed by Conquistadors Dominguez and Escalante. Supposedly, the explorers discovered a placer mine of gold in the Four Corners area, but its exact location was not known publicly. One of the versions of the story was that there was a large silver mine above where this big strike was scored.

Then in 1876, while patrolling in the Four Corners area near Cortez, two American soldiers, cavalrymen named Merrick and Mitchell were riding high up on a butte where few people ever rode. They discovered a crude forge, and discovered a number of gold and silver nuggets nearby.

Some of the local Navajos spotted the two soldiers and knew what they had discovered and warned the two men to leave the area and stay away. Merrick and Mitchell left, but they returned in less than a week and sneaked into the area at night, taking a number of samples of the ore. They took it to an assayer in Cortez, and the ore was valued at $800 per ton. In 1879, a businessman in Cortez named Jim Jarvis financed a mining company for the two men for half interest in the mine.

The two men did not want to wait for security and other mine workers to be hired, because they were so excited about possible riches. They sneaked back into the area to try to get some more ore samples.

After several days, they did not return, so Jim Jarvis alerted authorities and a search party was organized and sent out to look for them. They had gotten to the ore, but they were found at the bottom of a gulch, the ore spilled on the ground around them, their bodies riddled with Navajo arrows.

The search party spent even more time trying to find the entrance to the mine and searched the whole area for a long time, but found not a trace. They finally concluded that the Navajos, angry at the pilfering, started a rock slide and covered up the entrance to the mine.

A few years later, a priest in Prescott, Arizona Territory, told the story of meeting a dying man in a hospital in Denver, Colorado. The man told him that he and two other men had taken $75,000 worth of gold from a placer mine they found not far from Cortez on the big Navajo reservation in the Four Corners area. They got the gold but were discovered by some Navajos, who attacked them. According to the man, they fought their way out then and traveled south through New Mexico, crossing the Mogollons, then following the Gila River all the way to Verde, and from there they went on to Prescott.

He told the priest that his two partners both died while they were making their hurried trip through New Mexico and Arizona territories, and he was left with the gold. The man went on to say that he felt certain he was being followed by the Navajos and members of the spirit world, and he felt he was cursed as long as he kept the gold with him.

He had found a boulder that was shaped like a kneeling man outside of Prescott, and buried the gold at the base of the boulder. He wanted nothing more to do with the cursed gold, so he told the priest that he had carved a cross over a half circle in a tree a few paces from the spot where he buried it. He then told the priest that he wanted him to go and retrieve the gold himself and use the funds for the good of the hospital.

The priest actually went and found the tree and cross, but never found the buried chest full of gold. And nobody had found the Navajo gold and silver mine near the Four Corners area since.

Colt poured both men another cup of coffee and lit up cigarettes.

"You think these men found that gold?" Colt asked.

"It is one thing that might be," Man Killer said.

"Let's hope so," Colt said.

"Why do you say that?" Man Killer said.

Chris smiled over a sip of coffee, saying, "Well, they'll have to suffer with the curse of the Navajo, won't they?"

Man Killer grinned.

Both men mounted up and headed toward the San Juan River. They were only two hours from the river when they ran into the giant posse, which was headquartered near where Montezuma Creek ran into the San Juan. It was even hotter there than it had been in Cross Canyon.

The sheriff who was in charge was a slight, balding man who wore a handlebar mustache. His name as Marvin Laker. He had a tent set up in the shade not far from the San Juan. Two Navajo women had cooking fires going and were busy making fry bread, which was being picked up and eaten by posse members as fast as it was ready. There were a number of lawmen and want-to-be hardcases sitting around, drinking coffee and eating fry bread.

An old Navajo man walked up to Colt and Man Killer. Straight-faced, the man looked at Colt's big paint and said, "That is a Navajo horse. Why is a white man riding him?"

"The Navajo who have tried to ride him always fall out of the saddle."

The old man grinned, then got serious, "You were the man who took our friend home to his family so he could walk the spirit trail."

Colt gave Man Killer an astonished look, but the Nez Perce just grinned.

"How did you even know about this so quickly?" Colt asked.

"I know many things," the old man said. "My name is Ahkeah. You are Colt, and you are Man Killer of Those With Noses Who Are Pierced."

Chris got off his horse and reached inside his saddlebags, pulling out an oilskin pouch of tobacco, which he handed to the old man.

"This will help you with some of your ceremonies." Chris said. "Are you a shaman?"

The old man nodded, saying, "I am."

"What can you tell me?"

"Talk to the white eyes chief yonder," the old man said. "Then we will talk."

Chris nodded and walked away with his companion, saying, "S'pose we ought to go introduce ourselves to the sheriff and see what's going on."

Colt noticed that most of the men milling around seemed unorganized, and didn't know what to do. He wondered why daylight was burning and so many men were still around the headquarters and not out searching. The two men walked up to the sheriff and offered handshakes.

"Sheriff, I understand you're in charge here," Colt said.

The lawman acted impatient, but said, "Yes, hello, name is Marvin Laker. What can I do for you?"

"My name is Chris Colt, and this is my partner, Man Killer. We used to be lawmen, and we also worked as scouts for the cavalry. Came down to track these characters for you. More important, they have kidnapped my sister."

"Colt. Yes, I've heard of you—both of you in fact," Laker said. "First of all, sorry to say this, but if they kidnapped your sister, they've already killed her. As far as the tracking goes, thanks, but you're not a lawman now, and we have some really good trackers with us. In fact, I'm pretty much of a hand as a tracker myself.

So, thank you both for coming, but we don't need your help."

Colt felt his ears burning and could feel his blood pressure rise until he thought his face was going to explode off his skull.

Colt gritted his teeth and tried to control his temper until he could stand it no longer, finally saying, "Yeah, Sheriff, you sure couldn't use our help. You've done such a fine job of catching these killers. Why would you need a couple of expert trackers? And thanks so much for your concern about my sister."

The sheriff now grew red in the face and said, "How about if I just throw you in the hoosegow, Colt?"

"For what charge? Speaking my mind?" Colt challenged. "Last I heard, Americans were allowed to do that."

The sheriff said, "This is my county. I'll throw you in jail on any charge I want."

Colt's lips curled back. "You know what, Sheriff Laker, saying that you're going to put me in your jail and doing it are two different things. One is easy to do. The other thing is going to be a whole lot harder. Now, we came a lot of miles to help find some mad-dog killers who shot a lawman and kidnapped my sister. Are you interested in getting as much help as you can, or just in the glory of getting the killers yourself?"

The sheriff gritted his teeth, and his veins bulged. He turned on his heel and began to storm away. He abruptly stopped, his shoulders slumped, and he turned around and came back.

He was more relaxed now, saying, "Look, Colt, I'm a little on edge with this big thing going on, and I'm fighting with the Pinkertons and the cavalry. I need help, but just stay out of our way. The outlaws were spotted west of here yesterday, toward the bluff along the river. They're hiding in the thick brush, so we're going to burn them out."

Colt's mouth almost dropped open. "The brush?' Chris said. "This is springtime. Everything along the river is green. You aren't going to flush them out, you're going to signal them where you are."

Colt didn't believe he had ever heard of anything so stupid in law enforcement.

The sheriff's face got red again as he said, "Well, I know what I'm doing, and we have already started the fires. See the smoke?"

Colt said, "With this many men, if you know they are hiding along the river, you can just put a blocking force across the river on this side of the bluff, put out riflemen who are good shots all along both sides of the river at vantage points, then send another force down the river starting from here, walking side by side through the thick stuff. They won't get away."

"Just stay out of our way," the sheriff warned.

"Yeah, we'll check east of here."

"Famous tracker, huh?" The sheriff laughed. "They were spotted west of here, remember?"

Colt pointed at the thick smoke rising up into the sky from the little bit of dry brush that there was down in the valley.

"That's why they're going to be east of here," Chris said. "They're not going to stick around watching you trying to burn green brush. Nice meeting you, Sheriff."

Colt and Man Killer returned to where they left the horses.

"That man and others like him are why there are outlaws," Man Killer said.

"That's for damned sure," Colt replied.

Chris Colt did not often swear, saving it for special occasions such as this that involved gross stupidity and extreme frustration.

"Do you think they would go east?" Man Killer asked. "It would be easy to float on logs down the river toward the bluff."

"Well, the way I figure," Colt replied, "you are absolutely right. All the signs the sheriff found says they went west, but these guys didn't get as far as they have by not being able to hide their tracks."

Man Killer said, "We have not spoken of it, but you know they must have cached the Gatling gun somewhere else."

"Of course," Colt said, tightening his cinch strap, "but I think it is more important that we find them."

Three men, all wearing badges, walked up to Colt and Man Killer just then, trying to look intimidating.

"Who are you with?" one of them demanded.

Colt pointed at Man Killer saying, "I'm with him."

Man Killer grinned and pointed back at Colt, saying, "And I'm with him."

The three men walked away grumbling while the two trackers climbed into their saddles and rode toward the bridge across the river, spotting the lawmen out of the corner of their eyes. They were talking to other posse members, apparently relaying the frustrating conversation they just had.

Colt and Man Killer smiled to themselves as they felt the eyes of the posse on their backs. A couple of the posse members knew who the two were and were duly in awe. The others felt like

Colt and Man Killer were just outsiders, and did not want anyone there that was not one of their own.

The two crossed the bridge over the river and turned left on the far side. There was a cut-bank, actually more of a short cliff, to their right about fifty feet high, running for about a mile, before leveling off in a rolling, desert terrain with clumps of brown bunchgrass, mesquite, cacti, creosote, and plenty of rocks and sand.

Along the river, Colt and Man Killer picked their way through Russian olive trees, manzanita, and several types of thorny trees. In some places, the undergrowth along the river was so thick they could hear the water running just a few feet away but could not see it.

They rode into an area that was so thick that their horses could not see more than a few feet in any direction. The farther they rode into it, the thicker it got. The ground was covered with what woodsmen called tanglefoot, and though the trees were not over forty feet high, they were immensely thick.

Colt couldn't even see Man Killer, only a few feet away, but he heard a commotion. He patted War Bonnet's neck, and the big paint seemed to relax a little, although his nostrils were flaring wildly and his ears were twitching in every direction.

"Hawk is panicked," Man Killer yelled.

"Come to my voice," Colt said, "and we'll lead you out of this."

Colt started counting slowly, and within a minute, Hawk appeared from the giant thick green blades of brush. He touched noses with War Bonnet and seemed to calm down a little.

Colt pulled back gently on the reins and squeezed his calves against the pinto horse's ribs.

"Back, back," Colt urged. "Good boy."

War Bonnet backed up, his muscular rump pushing the gigantic weeds out of the way behind him. Hawk stayed right in front of the paint's nose, following him, while Man Killer kept petting him, telling him to relax.

After several minutes, War Bonnet emerged into a relatively clear area, and Hawk followed immediately. The big Appaloosa was drenched with sweat, and he was breathing heavily. The horse was even lathered between his legs and under his chest.

Man Killer dismounted and petted the big horse, then walked over to War Bonnet and grabbed his head, kissing him on the nose. Colt started laughing. The horses needed to rest so they wouldn't bind up. Colt stripped the saddle off his horse, and Man Killer removed Hawk's, so both steeds could get more relaxed. Hawk was still breathing heavily.

Chris gathered some dry creosote wood and made a small smokeless fire, then put on a coffeepot and stuck a frying pan in the fire.

"Might as well eat lunch early. Let the horses rest up."

Man Killer agreed.

After lunch, they pressed on, but avoided going into any more thickets like the one that panicked Hawk. The two trackers kept finding small paths into the trees and thick brush along the river. They apparently had been made by Navajos coming to the river to get water for their families, or maybe to fish. They also found tracks of sheep that used the trails to water. At each trail, the two men would bend down and walk by the tracks to the river's edge and look around. About a mile and a half east of the Montezuma Creek headquarters, Colt and Man Killer found the first tracks of the outlaws.

Leaving their horses behind, they walked stooped-over through the thick foliage to the river's edge. Less than fifty paces across the water was a long island, also covered with thick greenery. Looking into the shallow water leading to the island, Colt first spotted the tracks and pointed them out. Boot tracks showed in the sand under the water, which was crystal clear and less than a foot deep. The four outlaws were walking down the river in the shallow water at its edge, but when the water got deeper, they carefully stepped up on shore, walking on rocks or clumps of grass to avoid leaving footprints. They also had wrapped burlap or some kind of cloth around their feet in a further effort to hide their tracks. The water was much stiller here, and the current hadn't erased the tracks yet, which the two men estimated were only a day old. Colt and Man Killer, without having to speak of it, both understood what the bad men had done. They had walked along the river's edge, probably carrying their boots in their hands and just wearing their makeshift moccasins, letting the current eventually erase their tracks in the soft sand.

Man Killer pointed and said, "Look."

The faint tracks led across the little waterway out onto the island. Colt and Man Killer shed their boots and waded across to the island. In the island's interior, they found a sleeping area and an old campfire. The two men found where the outlaws had set down rifles and saddlebags.

"I'm not sure they are ex-military," Colt said.

"Because they did not stack arms?" Man Killer said, referring to the army's habit of stacking their rifles butts down in a circle, with the barrels resting against each other in the form of a teepee.

"We'll have to just keep watching for other clues, but I don't believe this is a military unit, or even deserters," Colt said. "Some old habits are hard to break. Charley must be with the Gatling gun, wherever that's cached."

"It is hard to tell from such little sign," Man Killer said.

"I know," Colt replied. "It's more of a hunch than anything."

Man Killer nodded. He knew that hunches provided some of the biggest pay-offs when an experienced tracker is on a trail. There is something about one's sixth sense in such a situation, probably related to one's concentration being at its peak, the mind constantly analyzing bits of information, sometimes subconsciously. But it is all to one great end, often providing the solution about where the quarry is going or has gone.

The two men now rode along the river a little farther out, because they knew the outlaw's tracks would keep leading up the river for a ways. The one chance they were taking was that the men might have swum across the river at some point. They didn't think so, though. It was safer for the outlaws to stay on the south side of the river and keep traveling east to get away from the other searchers.

After the two men passed where McElmo Creek poured into the San Juan from the north, they noticed that the rolling desert on their right now became cliffs again, and they were rising higher and higher.

"I have an idea," Chris said.

"What?" Man Killer replied.

"Let's swing over to our right more," Colt said. "It'll be easier on the horses. The vegetation's not as bad, and I have an idea those varmints might want to hole up along those cliffs or mesas to our right. If they get up higher, they can see what's going on, but can still stay close to the river for water. Maybe there's some caves up in those rocks."

"The People Who Came Before lived here in this area. There will be many hideouts," Man Killer replied.

"You mean the Anasazi?" Colt asked.

"Yes. I promise you we will find cliff dwellings along some of the cliffs," Man Killer said. "We must look very hard under places where the cliff juts out to make shade for the side of the mountain."

"Make shade for the side of the mountain? Partner, I can tell you are from the band of Chief Joseph," Chris replied. "Most folks would have said we need to look under overhangs. If we ride over where it is easier going, all we'll have to do is cut their trail from the river to the rocks."

In less than an hour, Man Killer spotted a dim trail in the sand where the outlaws had walked and then sprinkled sand over their tracks. But an experienced tracker could spot such a trail, when most others would not. It was something Chris Colt and Man Killer both knew—a man hiding his trail still left a trail every time. It was just not as obvious to see.

Colt and Man Killer rode the horses under some trees and spent the next hour looking up with binoculars at the sides of the cliffs. Behind them, across the river a mile away, were a sprinkling of Navajo hogans. The place was called Aneth. The hogans were earthen lodges fashioned over a frame of logs and branches. Colt and Man Killer spotted a Navajo sweat lodge not far in front of them, but as they scanned the ground they could tell the area had not been disturbed in some time. There was even a tumbleweed against the lodge's door, which looked like it had probably been there for some time.

Suddenly, in the side of a cliff, not too high up, Colt spotted what looked almost like a small brick wall.

"Man Killer—there, maybe fifty feet above the canyon bottom under those small overhangs. It looks like a wall under the overhang, and there's another one right past it. See it?"

Man Killer looked to where Colt's glasses were aimed, and he fixed his own on the area.

"Yes, I see," Man Killer said. "How do we keep from getting shot out of our saddles?"

Colt laughed. "Go back to that dandy house, grab two of those women, and get the heck out of the country. I hear Paris is beautiful this time of year."

Man Killer chuckled but kept looking through his glass, saying dryly, "You are a great tracker and mighty gunfighter, but you need to tell new jokes, not the same old ones."

"But that was your joke," Colt replied. "Did you spot the sheep trail that runs along the base of the cliff? Or at least I assume it's a sheep trail."

"Yes," Man Killer said.

"We can ride our horses right along that trail, and they will not see us until we are on top of them," Colt said. "They can see the whole valley from there, but not the base of the cliff running up to them. We can hide the horses down the bend from them, climb up, and put the sneak on them from above."

"But if they have hidden there," Man Killer said, "they would have seen us already."

"You're right," Colt replied. "We'll ride back downriver at an angle, so it looks like we gave up after coming this far. Then we'll turn back when we reach the trail along the cliff bottom."

They did so, but upon arriving at the base of the cliff, both men dismounted and stared at the trail. They saw the tracks of five shod horses heading toward the cliff dwelling, and the return tracks of the same five horses heading back down the trail. Both men noted that the tracks of the four led horses going upriver were not as deep as all five going back downriver. They had men in their saddles.

A voice made them both whirl and draw their guns.

It was that of Ahkeah, who walked out from among the rocks, saying, "You see they have gone."

"Get around, don't you, Ahkeah?" Colt said to his old shaman friend.

Ahkeah grinned. "I shape-shifted to search up and down the river for those men who would bring danger and many white-eyes to my people."

"Huh?" Colt said, not understanding.

Man Killer whispered, "I will explain later."

"They go beyond those who are fools down the river," the old shaman said. "It is almost dark. If you stay in the sacred dwelling, it will be cooler tonight. Your horses will like it better below. You will be near the river."

"Why do you help us instead of the sheriff?" Chris asked.

"You know the answer to such a question, Colt," the shaman replied, grinning. "When you pass this way again, we will do a sweat lodge together."

The old man was talking about a very spiritual ceremony to him, but Chris Colt was glad the old man offered to do it later on. The last thing he and Man Killer needed to do now was have their minds clouded up by smoking peyote, which the shaman would refer to as medicine. Chris grinned, tipping his hat. He and Man Killer mounted up and rode back toward the cliff dwellings they had spotted.

The Anasazi ruins were in two small cliffs under a low overhang. They left their horses down below, and carefully climbed up a notch in the front of the cliff. They then walked across the ledge and could see the ruins fully now. Both ruins were well over a thousand years old, but well-made and preserved by arid conditions, they looked like they could have been made only a year before.

The Anasazi,—the cliff-dwellers—had made bricks that looked like adobe, and simply erected walls along the front of the two cave openings. Each wall had two or three square windows built into it and an open area at the top so smoke could be let out. Climbing into the first one, both men saw that the four outlaws had indeed hidden out there. The sand floor was disturbed, and the remains of a fresh fire darkened the floor. There were scratches on the rock walls where guns had scraped against them in the cramped conditions. The three windows gave them a view of the whole valley where they could see just about anyone approaching by the logical routes.

Colt and Man Killer went below and stripped the saddles from their horses, stowing them under a tree. They retrieved the saddlebags, canteens, and whatever they would need for the night.

Over dinner, Man Killer looked at the flames of the small fire, saying, "Now I am more puzzled."

"This was all planned, this hideout," Colt said. "The outlaws knew they were coming to the San Juan River."

"And they have another who brought them horses," Man Killer replied.

"You said you'd explain later about what the old man said about . . . shape-shifting, was it?"

"The Navajo believe that some holy men, such as Ahkeah, can shape-shift," Man Killer replied. "They can change into an animal like a deer, owl, eagle, or coyote, and can explore or move around and then change back into a Navajo. In their ceremony when they smoke medicine and leave the lodge, they do not think the same way as when they do not smoke. So some think that maybe they change into the spirit of an animal and look around through the animal's eyes and that their bodies really stay right there in the lodge."

"What do you believe?" Colt asked.

Man Killer replied, "I believe in God, the Father Almighty, Maker of Heaven and earth, and of Jesus Christ, His only Son, our Lord, who was conceived by the Holy Ghost, born of the . . ."

Colt interrupted, "Yes, I know the rest, Parson Man Killer, and I know you grew up going to mission school, and apparently you did not fall asleep in class. I just wanted to know what you felt about the shape-shifting."

"I believe a man is stupid to keep his mind closed to the ideas and beliefs of other men," Man Killer answered. "What do you believe?"

"I believe you are wise well beyond your years, brother."

The next morning after breakfast, the two men saddled up and trotted back down the valley toward the headquarters of the sheriff, who had not impressed them very much. When they rode up to the chief lawman, he was in a heated discussion with a cavalry major and a man clad in an expensive suit and derby. The sheriff left the discussion to turn to Colt and Man Killer.

"Where were you two last night?" Sheriff Laker fumed. "Why didn't you check in? I can't spare men to go looking for others who don't show up at night."

Colt looked around and said, "It looks to me, Sheriff, like you can't spare men to go looking for murderers or kidnappers, either. We spent the night in the hideout the outlaws stayed in the night before along the south side of the river."

"How can you be sure?" the sheriff snapped.

"Someone met them yesterday with four

horses, and the five of them rode out headed this way, traveling along the south side of the river," Colt replied.

"Well, Colt," the sheriff snapped, "I'm sure you think you're right, but I believe we're going to flush them out by burning the brush along the river."

Man Killer smiled and said, "And I believe that if I stay up long enough this Christmas, I will finally get to see Saint Nicholas."

Five men wearing badges came riding in, and one seemed very excited. They were leading a long-legged steeldust gelding. The excited man jumped off his horse and ran up to the sheriff as the man in the derby and the cavalry major walked over to join them.

The excited man said, "Sheriff, we found this steeldust gelding wandering along, grazing just above the bluff toward Blanding. He was eating grass along the stage road. I bet your fire flushed them outlaws out."

The sheriff had a look of triumph on his face. He smiled first at the major and the derby-hatted man, then at Colt and Man Killer. The major's patrol began to pack up and get into the saddle, ready to ride out.

"This steel dust was positively identified as one of the horses the outlaws were riding." The sheriff beamed. "The great Chris Colt here just tried to tell us that they found a hideout eight miles upstream where the killers hid until yesterday."

Man Killer walked over to the steeldust and looked at the horse's legs. He summoned Colt over with a crooked finger. Chris approached, so the rest followed suit. Man Killer pointed to bloody scabs on the bottom of the horse's two forelegs. He then pulled a long wooden splinter out of one of them. Colt nodded in understanding.

"Did he say you were Chris Colt?" the cavalry major asked.

Colt nodded, and the major pumped his hand. "Pleased to meet you, sir. I have served with a number of fine officers who speak very highly of you. And you as well, sir. You must be Man Killer. I am Major Randolph Dillinger."

He vigorously shook with the Nez Perce warrior, too.

"Major, why would the cavalry have somebody of your rank out here helping look for these killers along with a large-sized patrol, judging by your campsite?" Colt asked.

The major cleared his throat and shuffled his feet tensely. "Mr. Colt," the major replied, "the army wants to be a good neighbor to our civilian friends in the territory."

"Major, I'm not a newspaper reporter," Colt said grinning. "Why are you really here?"

"Just being neighborly, like I said," the major said. "Plus we want to get our Gatling gun back."

"I know that, but you can do it without a major leading a large patrol. What do you have, about forty men?"

The major shuffled nervously again and didn't answer this time.

The sheriff chimed in, "Yeah, why are you here, *major*, and why is your patrol so large? You're not after Geronimo, are ya?"

"There just weren't any lower rank officers available," the major replied. "Say, what did you just determine from looking at the horse's forelegs?"

"The horse scraped himself jumping out of a man-made corral," Colt stated. "The men probably stabled the horses somewhere in that area and were planning on coming back to them. I'll bet the Gatling gun and my sister are within a stone's throw of where their horses are stabled, too."

"Balderdash!" the sheriff exclaimed.

"Sheriff Laker," the major cut in, "these two

men scouted with Al Sieber, Colt scouted for Custer—"

"He sure did Custer a lot of good, didn't he?" the sheriff interrupted.

Colt smiled and said quietly, "Sheriff, Custer died because he was a hardheaded idiot who didn't want to listen to people with experience. He put his ego and his own selfish interests above the welfare of those he was in charge of."

You could hear a pin drop. Nobody said a word, least of all Sheriff Laker, who turned on his heel and stormed away. The major pulled a green scarf from his trouser pocket and wiped the sweat off his face. Colt noticed this, but didn't show it.

"Well, Mr. Colt, guns are not the only thing you are fast and shoot straight with," the major said chuckling. Then getting more serious, he said, "I am afraid, sir, that the chances of your sister being alive with those cutthroats are slim. What are you going to do now?"

"Rescue my sister, get the killers, and recover the Gatling gun," Colt staid. "I disagree about Charley's chances because our family, Major, is quite wealthy. We love our sister dearly and would pay anything for her safe return. I'd even drop the whole thing with the outlaws if she hasn't been harmed and she's returned safely."

"I wish I was authorized the funds to hire you to scout for our patrol. But let me know if and when you recover the Gatling gun," the major said. "I have to get it back to Wyoming. I am heading up north now. I was only given so many days to be out. Good luck."

They watched as the major and his men headed west along the north side of the river. At the bluffs, they would turn north. It was the exact route Colt planned to take.

Colt and Man Killer started to ride out of the encampment, but several men with deputy's badges suddenly blocked their way with their horses. The sheriff walked over to them, his jaw set firmly.

"Take their guns, boys," Sheriff Laker said. "Colt, Injun, you're both under arrest."

Colt and Man Killer drew all four guns before anybody could move. One deputy started to draw, but Colt fired, and the man's hat flew backward. Everybody froze.

"What charge?" Colt asked.

"Obstructing justice."

"Where did you learn that terminology, Sheriff Laker?" Colt said. "I didn't think you had any knowledge about the law at all. You know, the way you are trying to keep us from catching these killers and rescuing my sister, someone might think you have some interest in them *not* getting caught. Why do you have so many posse members around here all the time, instead of having them go looking for the outlaws?"

The sheriff's face turned crimson, but now he was on the defensive.

"That is preposterous!" Laker raged. "I just don't need any busybody know-it-all ex-lawmen around here trying to tell me how to do my job, and trying to take the credit for capturing those killers."

Laker turned and stormed away to his tent to pout some more. Colt and Man Killer holstered their guns and started walking their horses away. The major was already at the head of his patrol, heading downriver. Colt and Man Killer headed in the same direction. They wanted to backtrack the deputies who brought in the steel-dust, and then trace the horse back to the corral.

It only took a half an hour for Colt and Man Killer to overtake the cavalry patrol. They made brief conversation with the major before continuing on, wanting to hurry. Colt felt that the outlaws were going to cross the river and take this road to a town called Bluff, where the stable where their horses were kept surely was located.

After leaving the cavalry patrol behind them,

Man Killer asked Colt, "Why did you place bait to trap the major?"

"Bait?" Colt replied. "What bait?"

Man Killer mocked Colt sarcastically, "We would pay anything for my sister's safe return. I would drop the whole thing if I had to."

"I don't trust him totally," Colt replied.

"Why?"

"A hunch," Colt said. "Tell you later if it pans out."

They were a few miles outside Bluff when Ahkeah appeared, coming out from a cut running down to the river, smoking a pipe. He held up his hand, and the two men rode up to him. They dismounted and let their horses take a blow.

Man Killer spotted a small brown-and-white Tobiano pinto pony down below in the cut. He was grazing on a long tether line, and was wearing a war bridle. Man Killer gave Colt an almost imperceptible look and signaled with his eyes, directing the tracker's glance to the cut. Colt spotted the pony and almost smiled.

They shook hands with the old man. Colt dove into his saddlebags and gave the man a pouch of tobacco.

The old man placed something in Colt's saddlebag. He turned to the tracker, saying, "A gift for your little girl."

"You sure do get around, Ahkeah," Colt said. "You have strong medicine."

Ahkeah said, "See where the road turns yonder?"

"Yes."

"To your left, you will see a trail," the shaman said. "It leads down the river to a bridge. You will leave your horses. On the other side, behind all those trees, there is a dwelling from the People-Who-Came-Before. It has many rooms."

He held up his hands twice showing the number sixteen.

"The white men you seek stayed there last night," he went on. "Maybe they are there now, but I do not think they are."

"Obliged," Colt replied. "I will see you again sometime."

"Yes," Ahkeah said, "in two years, I think."

He turned and walked back toward the cut without another word, as mysterious as ever. Neither man let him know that they saw his horse hidden there. Ahkeah did not let them know how sore the old bones and muscles in his legs and back were from riding so hard and so fast. It was much more important to Ahkeah to let them think he had very powerful medicine, since they were such great warriors, spoken about in the lodges of many different nations.

As they watched him disappear into the cut, Man Killer smiled at Colt. "Do you think he knows we saw his horse?"

"Nope," Colt replied, "and I'll bet you he soaks in some hot water tonight, too. He's probably as sore as a man who wrestled with a bull buffalo, as hard as he had to be riding today."

"Why does he hide these things, do you suppose?" Man Killer asked.

"You know why," Colt replied. "Crazy Horse always wore war paint the same way when he went into battle, as most Indians do. He always wore a hawk feather hanging down at an angle in the back of his hair, hung a pebble behind his left ear, and wore one decorated sheep skin anklet on his left shin."

Interested, Man Killer said, "Yes?"

"The thing that all the Lakotah and Cheyenne admired about Crazy Horse was that he claimed to be so close to the Great Spirit that he could not be wounded in battle. He would charge people all the time in battle and ride back and forth, challenging the enemy to shoot at him."

Again, Man Killer said, "Yes?"

"The reason Crazy Horse wore the one anklet on his left leg was to hide the scar from the bullet hole in his leg," Chris said.

"And among his own people, he was a bigger legend than among the white man," Man Killer said.

Colt nodded, adding, "Because they all thought he had such powerful medicine, being so close to the Great Spirit as he was."

The two men mounted up and headed toward the road to Bluff. The road cut between some rocks, and there was indeed a trail leading toward the river. They rode down to the river as the trail dropped down the face of a cliff about seventy feet above the river. A foot bridge suspended across the water was swinging back and forth in the wind. Colt and Man Killer dismounted, grabbing their carbines from their scabbards.

The bridge crossed the fast-moving river, and disappeared into a vast tangle of green trees and foliage on an island.

Slinging their rifles upside down to avoid snagging them on the thick foliage stretching across the bridge, they went across as quickly and as quietly as possible, although being stealthy moving across a swinging suspension bridge was a difficult task, at best.

On the other side, they simply followed the well-worn trail, which took them right up to the base of the rusty red cliff and the giant Anasazi ruin built into the naturally scooped-out bowl in the side of the cliff. The two men carefully drew their Peacemakers and entered the ruins. Searching through them room by room, they discovered the abandoned cooking fire of the outlaws and the remains of their meals. Walking outside, they found where the outlaws had ridden all the way down and forded the river, apparently swimming with their horses to the other side.

The two trackers saddled up on the other side of the river, and went out after the killers, picking up their tracks where they climbed up the steep hillside. The trail, as expected, was clearly heading toward Bluff. The cliffs on the other side of the river rose higher, so by the time the pair were just outside Bluff, the cliffs were several hundred feet high. Between the cliffs on their right, however, was an opening, and a narrow canyon opened up heading due north toward the towns of Blanding and Moab. The road forked, and the outlaws seemed to have taken the right fork heading toward Blanding. The tracks were pretty fresh, so Colt and Man Killer knew they would close on the outlaws before too long.

They headed north, still wondering what was

in the minds of these killers. As they rode, they spoke their concerns.

"I still haven't figured out what's going on with them," Colt said. "I have a feeling that whatever they are up to is very important to the army. They don't have all that many majors in the cavalry to send one out in charge of a simple patrol."

"But maybe the commanding officer of the major just wants to make an example," Man Killer replied. "You and I have seen many commanders who will ride a long, hard trail just to win a small battle."

Colt thought for a minute, then said, "That's a real good point, Man Killer. It could just be that, but still it's a feeling I have."

"I do not believe now that it has to do with the Navajo gold and silver," Man Killer said. "The outlaws are riding in the wrong direction."

Dark was closing in, and the two decided to speed up their pace. They were still well south of Blanding when they found the turn-off where the killers attempted to eradicate their tracks. The trail went down into a crack among some rocks about fifty paces wide. They had used a branch to wipe the ground back and forth, covering their hoofprints. The problem for the outlaws was the trained eyes of Colt and Man

Killer, who spotted the cover-up simultaneously, seeing the faint marks of the brush being swept back and forth in a fan shape.

They dismounted and led their horses forward, holding their rifles in their hands. The sun was setting on the distant horizon. A short distance into the cut, they rounded a bend slowly, and saw the camp of the four outlaws. The Gatling gun, mounted on a small cart and facing out toward the entrance to the gulch, was very menacing. The rugged walls of the gulch would not allow the famed trackers to approach from above, or behind.

They backed off and whispered to each other.

"I did not see a guard," Man Killer said.

"The only way they can be approached is from the front," Colt said, "and they got that Gatling gun. We are going to have to be very careful."

"Should we wait until night?" Man Killer asked.

"We'll have to," Colt said. "If we try to go in there now, we'll get shot to pieces."

"I can ride back and get that major and the cavalry," Man Killer said.

"That's probably going to be our best bet," Chris replied, "but I am just not sure I trust him.

We do need help, though. I'll wait in those rocks over there.''

Man Killer led his horse away and mounted up out on the road, galloping back the way they had come. Colt slowly moved into the rocks with his big horse.

Delbert Monitor was Buzztail's real name, and he had one major problem besides being a sociopath: He had severe insomnia. Nightmares horrified him any time he went to sleep, so he had to walk around or sit and look up at the stars or at the campfire at night, until he just about passed out. Soon after, though, he would invariably sit up, shaking and sweating from a bad dream. This night, he decided to climb up the steps the Anasazi had chipped into the rock wall next to his camp. He sat on the cliff walls, looking up at stars until well past midnight. He was finally getting sleepy when he spotted a little patch of white that moved within a jumble of boulders near the wall. He moved closer and saw more white. It was part of a big black-and-white paint horse.

Chris Colt heard War Bonnet nicker a warning, and he sat up quickly, Peacemaker in his hand, but the click of the gun above him made him freeze.

"Easy buster," Buzztail said. "Let back on that hammer, and let the gun drop down easy, over toward the horse."

Colt's mind raced. He knew these killers would shoot him or torture him or Charley without blinking an eye. There had to be a way to get out of this jam.

Buzztail said, "Ease that gun down now, or I shoot with no more talkin'."

Colt let the gun drop slowly to the ground, praying for Man Killer to show up. Chris thought about the big Bowie hidden in the sheath down the back of his shirt. His gun belt was too far away to attempt a draw. If he could reach down the back of his shirt, maybe he could roll and throw.

"I recognize the horse," Buzztail said, "Chris Colt, ain't ya'?"

Chris didn't respond.

"Real slow, Colt. Left hand. Unbutton the shirt and take it off, slow-like," Buzztail said.

Colt felt his heart sink. After the shirt, the rest of his clothes had to come off piece by piece. And so it was that the mighty Chris Colt, legendary gunfighter, chief of scouts and tracker extraordinaire, was made to march into the encampment fully naked and vulnerable, hands clasped behind his head. His captor led the big pinto.

When Man Killer and the cavalry patrol arrived, he, the major, and three soldiers slowly walked forward, leaving their horses to meet with Chris Colt. Not finding him, Man Killer found his clothes and Bowie knife, left there by Buzztail. Man Killer cupped several lit matches near the ground and found the tracks, reading the story.

They returned to the patrol before anybody spoke.

"The smallest of the killers," Man Killer said, "the one they called Buzztail, caught Colt and took him prisoner. He is in their encampment. We must be careful. I can try sneaking up over the rocks to cut him and Charley loose."

"Sorry. I don't want to compromise my men by taking a chance on you getting caught, too," Dillinger said.

"What are you going to do?" Man Killer asked.

"I'll handle it," the major said, obviously put out by the challenge to his authority. "Don't worry. Sergeant Buck, bring your men up here. Sergeant Wilkins, bring yours, too."

Two sergeants came forward on their horses, leading almost the entire patrol, all but five men.

Both snapped to attention.

"You see the gap between the rocks?" the major said.

"Yes, sir."

"You two will take your men forward slowly, squads abreast, until you are within range of a surprise charge," the major said slapping his glove into his palm. "I don't want any cowards turning back. If you get in there quick, they'll never have time to get their hands on that Gatling gun. Save the woman and Colt first."

"You cannot do this," Man Killer protested. "They will kill Charley and Colt."

"I do not argue with subordinates in combat," the major said roughly. "Sergeant, take his guns, gag him, and tie him up. I don't want this operation compromised."

Several rifles were cocked, and Man Killer knew he was helpless for now. The majority of the patrol moved forward after a short pep talk from Major Dillinger. Man Killer's mind raced as he tried to think of a plan.

In the encampment, Buzztail looked at the hot iron he had placed in the fire, then turned and grinned at Chris Colt, his hands tied high up on a large tree trunk. Charley Colt, alive but haggard, was tied up next to Colt. Fully clothed, she shot relieved looks at her brother. Colt only hoped he could get them both out of this mess. Buzztail got up close to Colt, his face illuminated by the stoked fire. The other killers enjoyed seeing the sight of this legend in their grasp.

Buzztail whispered, "The high-and-mighty Chris Colt, huh? The iron ain't hot enough yet, but it's gonna be soon."

He laughed, wanting to revel in Colt's misery, but Chris acted nonchalantly.

"Why?" Colt replied. "Are you going to try to kill me while I'm tied up and then burn a notch in your gun."

The attempt did not work to get the little murderer's goat. Buzztail just laughed some more, then said, "Naw, we're gonna burn a notch or two in you and watch ya scream a whole lot."

"No, that's where you're very wrong, partner," Colt said. "You won't hear a peep out of me."

Colt meant it, too. He had been tortured before, even had to watch while the small finger on his left hand was sawed off with a knife. The pain was excruciating, but Chris Colt would not give his captors the satisfaction of hearing him scream.

Buzztail chuckled, saying, "Want to bet? Watch this."

With all the other stress, Chris Colt was extremely humiliated at being tied naked to a post next to his sister. But what happened next only served to fuel Colt's helplessness. Buzztail walked up to Charley grinning, and opened her blouse, fondling her breast. Charley closed her eyes, biting her lower lip.

"I'm going to kill you, you son of a bitch!" Colt screamed. "Let her alone!"

He didn't yell just in anger. He hoped Man Killer and the cavalry could hear him and would know that Charley was still alive.

One of the others whispered, "Buzztail, here comes the patrol."

"Okay, you men know what to do," Buzztail said. "Get to your positions. Wait until the first shot."

Man Killer and the remaining five soldiers moved off to one side so no stray bullets could hit them. Then his rope was tied off to a stump while the major dismounted and shucked his rifle from its scabbard. The six men then moved forward. When the first patrol was almost at the entrance to the gulch, they stopped. The lead sergeant lifted a saber high in the air, the blade glistening in the moonlight. That is when Major Dillinger fired, shooting the sergeant through the back of the head. Immediately, his five troopers opened fire on the backs of the other men in the lead patrol, just as the Gatling gun and several rifles opened up from within the encampment. It was a slaughter. In seconds, all the patrol members, except those with Major Dillinger, lay dead along with many of their horses. Each was riddled with bullets. Man Killer could not believe it, and watching from within the camp, Colt and Charley were stunned as well. Seconds later, Colt was shocked again to see Man Killer being brought to his tree. The Nez Perce's hands were raised, and the manacles were taken off. His wrists were bound tightly, high up against the tree, just like Colt's.

Buzztail shook hands with Dillinger.

"Good work," Dillinger said. "Now burn the bodies."

Man Killer, Charley, and Colt watched in horror as several gallons of kerosene were poured on the corpses of the soldiers.

The fire was lit and Charley, Colt, and Man Killer tried to endure the smell of burning flesh. They heard a scream from somewhere within the pile of bodies. Apparently, one of the ambushed troopers had been playing 'possum. The men all watched as the bodies burned for a good while, then the major walked over and set his tunic down on the ground next to the smoking, charred heap.

"We're in a tight one this time, brother," Colt whispered.

Man Killer summoned courage, saying, "We will get out of this, somehow. We always have. Charley, you are like my sister. Do not worry about what we see."

She smiled, conscious of her still-exposed breast, "Thanks, Man Killer, but that is the least of my worries. I want you both to understand— if worse comes to worst, I may have to try something very desperate to give you both a chance to get loose."

"What do you mean?" Colt said, almost panicked.

"Chris," she said, "they have been making comments about what they want to do to me. Especially that ugly one over there with the missing ear. I may have to entice them to give you two some kind of distraction."

A tear appeared in Colt's right eye.

"I can't let you do that, Charley," Colt said. "For God's sake. You're my sister."

"We will do what we have to do to get out

of this," she said, her chin held up proudly. "And you two will have to see what happens to me if it does. You have to be strong-minded and think only about providing our escape. Do you both hear me?"

"You are a great woman, Charley," Man Killer said.

She stuck her chin up again, saying, "No. I am a Colt."

The major, now changed into cowboy clothes, walked over to them along with Buzztail. Ruby, Horace, and Big Ears were now relegated to the roles of gang members, with apparently no authority.

"I didn't know whether I should kill him or not," Buzztail said, "so I figgered to wait fer you."

"Good thinking, Del," Dillinger said. "Both of these men are extremely wealthy. Just a little extra for you and me. Don't mention it to the others. We can get quite a ransom for all of them."

"But, Major, we are gonna be filthy rich. We'll each have millions," Buzztail said.

Colt and Man Killer gave each other side-long glances.

The major chuckled, saying, "Delbert, my dear crooked, murderous compadre, you can never have enough money. Man Killer there is worth millions of dollars on his own. Colt and his sister are probably worth a million more."

Buzztail looked at them, grinning, "That Injun's worth millions?"

"Sure is," Dillinger said. "He married him a pretty young lady whose family was filthy rich, and she inherited it all."

"Well, he ain't stupid," Buzztail said. "Bet he poisoned all the family so's he could get his dirty little red hands on the money."

He paused for a minute, then said, "You know what? You took away my fun. I was gettin' ready to do a little torturin' the mighty Chris Colt here—and jest take a look at his sister. Thet's like watchin' a cherry pie cool off on the windowsill."

"Hey, Man Killer, is it just me," Colt taunted, "or do all the cowardly crooks I meet lately make war on women?"

Buzztail gritted his teeth and ran up to Colt, backhanding him across the jaw.

Colt spit blood in the man's face, saying, "I'm going to enjoy killing you, little man, and when I do, you'll have to stand up and face me like a man."

Buzztail stared daggers at Colt as he wiped the blood and spittle off his face. He started forward, pulling out his knife, but the major grabbed his forearm.

"Look, we have to let them all live to write ransom notes, and answer any letters to prove they're alive. But he doesn't have to be in top shape to do that," the major said. "I'll let you torture him tomorrow morning before we leave. And we'll both have some fun with the girl tonight. Okay?"

Buzztail got close to Colt's face, saying, "Tomorrow morning, you're gonna burn before our bacon does, boy. I could shoot you in a stand-up gunfight, I know I could, but it'll be more fun burnin' ya and hearin' ya scream."

Colt grinned at him, saying, "We'll see . . . boy."

Buzztail walked away, as did the major.

"Major Dillinger," Chris called out.

The man walked back over to Colt.

"You're going to be killing us anyway, so would you satisfy our curiosity?" Colt asked. "You must be a real genius to come up with such an intricate plan."

Man Killer and Charley both laughed to themselves when they heard Colt say this, knowing he was baiting the criminal into revealing his secret. They even noticed Dillinger's shoulders straightening back in pride when Colt said he was a genius.

Dillinger thought for a minute before saying, "I guess it won't hurt, because we are going to kill you three. If you all cooperate while you're alive, I will promise to kill you quickly."

Man Killer, who was not prone to joke, said sarcastically, "What a fine gentleman you are."

Colt started laughing and pretty soon even Dillinger joined in, as the irony struck him funny, too. Even Charley started giggling.

"I suppose it won't hurt to tell you. I was commanding a troop at Fort Laramie, and Buzztail was my orderly. I was in a meeting and learned that the army was going to try an experiment in consultation with the Pinkerton Agency. Do you have any idea how many millions of dollars in silver bullion are coming into the Denver mint each month? Guess what? Day after tomorrow, a specially built freight wagon with steel plating all around it, like a giant moving safe, will be crossing the Utah-Colorado border near Grand Junction with a fifteen-man cavalry escort carrying $10,000,000 in gold and silver bullion. Guess who will be waiting in the Utah badlands between Grand Junction and Green River with a Gatling gun?"

"And how many more of your own men are

you going to mow down with the Gatling before you are done?" Colt asked.

Dillinger grinned, saying, "Well, I am pretty good at arithmetic. Dividing a bunch of money by less people means more money for each person. What you should be worrying about is how bad you're going to get burned in a few hours. In fact," Dillinger said, turning to Man Killer, "I think I'll let Delbert work on you in the morning, too, my red-skinned friend with the sharp tongue."

Dillinger started to walk away, but turned and walked back, grinning and saying, "By the way, we left more evidence for the stupid sheriff back there near Montezuma Creek. You almost killed it for us. But the new evidence will keep him searching in that area for a while, and it will keep every available peace officer for miles around out of our way. They hate it so when you kill one of their kind. Pleasant dreams."

Colt, Charley, and Man Killer gave each other strained looks and worked at the thick ropes, but they were just too tight. Without warning, a blade suddenly came out of the darkness from behind the tree, and jutted between the faces of Colt and Man Killer. They both grinned as they saw it. It was the blade of a Japanese Samurai sword. Both men felt their hearts pounding with joy and newfound hope. They both recalled the time they saw that blade in action. Gunmen had been holding cocked pistols pointed at their backs in a saloon down in Trinidad. Tora, the former Samurai warrior who had lived with the Comanches, sprung into action, decapitating a gunfighter with his sword in the middle of a big shoot out.

Colt and Man Killer were both thinking about that night when they felt their arms drop free. Charley could barely contain her elation as she felt the freedom provided by Tora's scalpel-sharp Katana Samurai sword.

It was Justis Colt's voice behind them whispering in the darkness that gave the explanation. "Chris, Man Killer. Tora put the sneak on these outlaws and got your horses and gear. They're behind these trees. Charlotte, pleased to meet you, cousin. We'll talk more pleasantly later. You will have to lead the horses out the front of the gulch quietly. That's the only way. Charley, was your horse the big red chestnut stallion?"

"Yes," Charley whispered.

"Good. We've got him, too. Lead them, and we'll be up above and behind the outlaws to create a diversion. Maybe we can get them to swing the Gatling around. You'll only have seconds. Meet us downhill a mile. There's a cut that comes right up close to the road. Ride into it and hide your trail. Good luck."

"Thanks, cousin. Tora," Colt whispered.

Charley echoed, "God bless you both."

They heard the two sneak away into the darkness, then watched the guard by the fire who was occupied preparing a new pot of coffee. Slowly, Colt, Man Killer and Charley backed away into the shadows. In minutes, they had their guns strapped on and were leading their horses out toward the entrance of the little box canyon. As Chris's clothes were still outside the canyon in a pile, he wore his holsters and gun belt, but absolutely nothing else.

The trio walked next to their saddles and tried to stay in the shadows. They were almost parallel to the Gatling gun when the guard with the coffeepot spotted them and started to grab for his rifle. From up on the rocks, Justis's bullet took him through both hip bones. Then Justis and Tora started pouring shots into the campfire. Several men ran to the Gatling and swung it around.

Dillinger screamed, "Colt and Man Killer! They got away! They're up on that rock behind us. Get them!"

One of the killers opened up with the Gatling

gun and bullets sprayed all over the top of the rocks, but Justis and Tora were already down, scrambling for their horses.

Chris, Charley, and Man Killer grabbed their saddle horns and swung up into their saddles as the horses took off with a burst of speed. It took the killers completely by surprise, and they were a little slow in getting the crank-operated automatic Gatling turned around. Colt and Man Killer swung to the right, and Charley to the left, out of sight at the end of the box canyon entrance a split second before bullets cracked behind them.

The major, used to being in charge and taking command in an emergency, yelled, "Hurry, men! Strike camp! They'll have to organize the posse, and that will give us at least a ten-hour head start to get up north to intercept the wagon. I'll buy us all fresh horses in Moab! Let's go!"

As soon as the escapees met up with Justis and Tora, they jumped off their horses and shook hands heartily.

Colt who had stopped and grabbed his clothes outside the box canyon, now put them on amidst chuckles.

Climbing back up in the saddle, he said, "Come on. We're going to have to work fast to outwit them. You can tell us on the way how you two got here when you did."

As they rode north toward Moab, Justis explained, "I left the Texas Rangers a year ago and became a Pinkerton agent. Our company offered these armored freighter wagons the opportunity to carry a lot of gold and silver bullion to the Denver Mint. The company thought it might be a safer way, security-wise, than the railroad, and much more economical to the military. There is a test run of one million in silver coming from some of the mines in California and Nevada."

"They think that it's millions worth of gold and silver," Chris said.

"That was the original plan," Justis said, "but we decided that was too much money for an experiment, so it was cut back."

"What brought you here, though?"

"Stealing the Gatling gun was an inside job. We knew it had to be," Justis replied. "I started investigating and discovered that Private Delbert Monitor used to be this Major Dillinger's orderly. Dillinger court-martialed him for insubordination and tossed him out of the army right after a meeting where the major learned about our delivery plans. We checked on Monitor and learned that he had some nasty friends he associated with before going into the army, as well.

Meanwhile, as Monitor was linking up with his old outlaw friends, Major Dillinger had been investigated and cleared at two different army posts for missing funds from the post cup and flower fund, and from the payroll at the other post. Guess he figured that nobody in the army was going to compare notes from one duty station to the next. They all had one connection in Colorado that all communiques referred to as Mr. Green, but we believe that was a code name."

"I know who he is," Colt said. "I'll tell you about that later. We already heard from Dillinger that a wagon is coming across from Green River to Grand Junction the day after tomorrow with an escort of fifteen cavalry, which are supposed to get cut down in cold blood."

"No, there are several wagons and it is tomorrow," Justis corrected, "not the day after."

Colt looked back at Charley and Man Killer, who were fast-trotting behind War Bonnet.

"Looks like we get no sleep until tomorrow night," Colt said.

"You're right," Justis said. "It will be dawn very shortly."

"How are the five of us going to take out a Gatling gun?" Man Killer asked.

"Very carefully," Colt said, looking back, grinning.

Justis laughed, but Man Killer sighed, "All of his jokes are old. I have to hear them many times."

"If the wagon train is coming through tonight," Colt said, "we don't have to worry about the gold."

"I know," Justis responded. "We could never get up to the area between Green River and Grand Junction in less than two days of hard riding, but our genius criminal mind, the major, doesn't know that."

"Now all we have to do is bring some madmen killers to justice," Colt said.

"And get past many fast-flying bullets from that gun," Man Killer said. "How do we do that?"

"First, we have to get far ahead of them," Chris replied. "Let's stretch it out for a while. Then I have an idea."

It was rough on the major's men going around the town of Blanding, but they didn't want to draw any attention to the Gatling gun. They stopped briefly to eat north of town, then moved on.

It was near La Sal Junction, within sight of

Wilson Arch and Looking Glass Rock, that the
major and his men were forced to stop by a
large tree that had blown down, and was now
lying across the road. The horses could walk
over it, but the wagon had to detour around one
end and ride through a sandy area. The outlaw
driving the Gatling gun cart clucked to the
horses, and they swung around the end of the
tree. Suddenly, a thick spearlike stick was thrust
out from the inside of the green leafy part of
the fallen tree, and it caught right through the
spokes. The stick turned around a half revolu-
tion with the wheel and caught on the body of
the cart, halting its progress. The driver went
flying forward onto the trace harness and was
thrown to the ground underneath the wagon.
He started to crawl out with his gun in his hand,
and saw a pair of legs and moccasin-clad feet in
front of him. He looked up just in time to see
the glint of Tora's blade.

The next thing he knew, Charley Colt, covered
with leaves and twigs, sat up directly in front of
him and cocked two Colt Navy .36's in his face.

"Want to live long enough to hang?" she
asked.

He carefully nodded.

Tora ducked back into the leaves before anybody had a chance to fire at him. From there, he crawled under the log, where it was safer.

Justis, Chris, and Man Killer opened up in a cross-fire ambush from both sides of the road and started emptying saddles. Both the major's and Buzztail's horses were cut down in the ambush. Buzztail's leg was pinned under his horse. The major apparently hit his head and got knocked out cold when he fell with his dead mount.

Man Killer, Chris, and Justis came out of their hiding places behind the rocks on both sides of the road. Several outlaws were only wounded and were quickly disarmed. Holding guns on Buzztail, they commanded him to drop his weapons, then they went over to try and lift the horse off his legs. Just as they bent over, they heard a blood-curdling scream behind them.

They all turned with guns drawn to see Major Dillinger, who had started to shoot at them. Just then, Dillinger's arms, hands still holding the rifle, seemed to drop off his body onto the ground, blood spurting from the stumps just above both elbows. He looked at them, eyes opened wide, and started running down the road, screaming bloody murder. It was then that they could see Tora standing behind the major, his blood-darkened blade glistening in the sun.

They returned to cuffing the outlaws, and helped Buzztail out from under the horse. He rubbed his legs vigorously, trying to restore the circulation.

Colt got real serious, saying, "Now Buzztail— I made you a promise. Give him his gun."

Buzztail was very nervous and said, "Yeah, well, if I kill ya, they'll gun me down."

"No, they won't. They'll let you go," Colt said. "You draw whenever you want, but before you die, I want you to remember one thing: You never should have touched my sister."

Colt looked totally calm as Buzztail looked frantically all around. He wanted to run. He wanted to scream. His mouth was so dry, it felt like it was full of sagebrush. He felt his knees shaking, and he felt cramps tightening his stomach.

Colt, seeing the man's nervousness said, "Troubled, killer? It's something getting a preview of what hell is like, huh?"

Buzztail thought maybe he could still beat this man, but he looked directly over into the eyes of Charley Colt. She raised her hand, waving, saying, "Bye, bye."

Buzztail's eyes opened wide, and a little squeal came out of his mouth as his hand went down for his gun. Just as his hand touched the handle of the old .44, a bullet slammed into his chest, then another, and another. He felt himself being propelled backward and saw the sky passing overhead. An elephant was standing on his chest. He wanted to cry for his mommy, but then realized Pa had killed her when he was young. He had awakened in her bed, lying next to her cold body. He didn't want to go to sleep now and stay that way forever. He tried to cry out, but nothing came. Then everything went blank.

CHAPTER 7
Back Home

They stopped in Westcliffe, several days after turning the outlaws over to the Deputy U.S. Marshal in Moab. The four immediately went to the sheriff's office and had a meeting with Sheriff Schoolfield, telling him all that had transpired.

Then all of them, including two of Schoolfield's deputies, went to the mercantile owned by Daniel Yost. He greeted them himself when they entered.

"Gentlemen, Miss Colt," Yost said nervously. "What can I interest you in today?"

"Green scarves," Chris said.

Yost's eyes opened wide, and his hand streaked into his jacket but Tora crossed the room in two strides. As he did, Justis tossed a green scarf from a nearby rack, and Tora spun in a whirl of slashing steel, slicing the silk scarf in three pieces. Daniel Yost's hand froze inside the jacket, his hand wrapped around the handle of his own Navy .36 in the shoulder holster. He watched the pieces of green scarf, along with his grandiose plans, fall to the floor. Sweat popped out on his forehead.

Charley drew her gun, saying, "Ease it out of the jacket with just one finger and your thumb."

Resigned, Yost pulled the gun out and let it drop to the floor. A deputy put irons on him.

"Sheriff," Colt said, "if you check his books upstairs, you'll see that he gave away many green scarves from his shop. The inventory doesn't match the receipts. He used it to help outlaws in his employ identify each other when they met up. Mr. Yost here traveled around the territory the past ten years. He'd go into a town and incite people into starting up Vigilance Committees, then he'd pick those who seemed ruthless enough to work for him directly. He hired a number of killers to try to kill me, as well as three different marshals in the territory. He wanted us out of the way. His books upstairs will also show you a number of plans for major robberies besides the Gatling gun theft he had planned, using men all over the surrounding country in a major syndicate of crime and injustice. I hope nobody else gets that idea in this country."

As they started to lead Yost to the door, he turned and said to Colt, "How do you know what's in my books?"

Chris winked at the sheriff.

"I believe," Colt said, "they call it tracking."

When Chris, Charley, Justis, Tora, and Man Killer rode up the Coyote Run ranch road, it seemed like all their friends and neighbors were there to greet them. After hugging and shaking hands with everyone, Colt went over to his saddlebags and reached inside, pulling out the gift that Ahkeah had placed there—a turquoise-and-silver squash bracelet that almost encompassed Brenna's whole arm from her wrist up to her elbow.

Giving her a kiss, Colt said, "A gift for you, honey. You'll grow into it."

Colt was both touched and amazed when his son, again sounding wise beyond his years, said, "Yes, Pa, thanks to heroes like you five."

Everyone applauded.

The crowd gathered around and started congratulating Man Killer and the Colts. The word had spread all over the territory. Then a hush fell over the crowd as old Long-Legged Bear walked up slowly from the bunkhouse, nursing a steaming cup of hot coffee. He walked right up to Chris, all eyes on him.

Long-Legged Bear didn't even look up from his cup of coffee, saying, "Why would you search for Charley Colt when you could not even find one red horse?"

Everyone laughed, even the children, although they might not have known why they were laughing.

Colt's and Man Killer's faces both became beet red.

Long-Legged Bear added insult to injury by adding, "When you have people call upon you to find tracks, you should tell them, 'See my sister—she is the tracker in our family.' "

Everybody laughed like crazy again, and the two legends laughed at themselves this time.

Chris winked at Man Killer, thinking about the fuss everyone was starting to make about them being so great as trackers. Man Killer seemed to read his mind.

Man Killer joked, "We did not do everything. What else did Charley do?"

Joshua said, "Aw, nothing much. She rode the rails over west of Wolf Creek, rented a roan, and picked up the horse thief's trail. She ran into some yahoos that wanted her to stay, permanent-like. She got helped out of that situation by one of the Sackett brothers who happened to be wandering by. They sent those three gents packing barefoot south without a stitch of clothes on, let alone a horse.

"Then she caught the horse thief, a young Ute named Jimmy Blind Elk, who was the grandson of a mighty chief. She had him tied up nice and tight in the saddle and was taking him to the law in Durango, when she was confronted by a war party of Utes.

"It sounds like the chief was that cousin of Ouray that was so danged tough in the wars. Anyhow, this Jimmy character is the old chief's grandson, and he takes exception to our little genteel sister here taking his kin off to the hoosegow. She's ready to battle the whole Ute nation, and when he hears her name is Colt, he ups and shoots his own grandson deader than a buzztail in a meat grinder, and allows that the boy has disgraced his family by stealing from the Colts. He then lets Charley know that she and any other Colt always has the welcome mat out in Ute territory.

"Now, she runs into a little trouble with the gang of cutthroats, but it was just a ploy to find out what the big gang was doing with a stolen Gatling gun. So she lets herself get kidnapped and taken to Utah, protecting my new stallion the whole time.

"Then you and Chris here mess up and get yerselves captured, and to add insult to injury, Justis and Tora here had to save ya. But it was okay, cause our little sister, Charley, was there and rescued all of you and hoodwinked the whole durned gang, put half of them in the hoosegow, and the other half are pushing up desert flowers with their toes. Then she safely escorted you all back here and brought me my stallion safe and sound."

Everyone cheered and applauded again while Joshua gave a blushing Charley a big hug.

"Joshua," Chris said, "you've been hanging out with Long-Legged Bear way too much."

Long-Legged Bear chimed in again by saying, "Colt, maybe while sister tracks, you learn how to be good cook and floor scrubber."

Everyone just howled with laughter, with Joshua actually falling on the ground, tears running down his cheeks.

Colt sat on a wooden lawn bench, and Brenna sat on her pa's lap as friends and neighbors talked and drank sun tea.

"Did you all hear what happened with the mighty Colt and Daniel Yost in Westcliffe?" Man Killer said.

Colt looked across the way at Mandy Morelli, and she kept glancing at him, averting her look when caught. Then he stared in wonder at the old Crow.

Long-Legged Bear said, "The mighty Colt found that Yost was the chief outlaw."

Chris said, amazed, "You've been here the whole time. It just happened. How did you ever know?"

The old man said, "Did you listen when I spoke?"

"Are we going through another one of your question-and-answer games?" Colt asked.

"Do you think we will?" Long-Legged Bear asked back.

Exasperated, Colt said, "We are!"

Long-Legged Bear said, "If you already know the answer, then why did you ask that question?"

Everyone laughed uproariously again, especially at Colt's growing frustration.

Chris said, "What was your question?"

Long-Legged Bear said, "Which question?"

"I don't know which question, you old coot! That's why I'm asking you!"

"A coot is a duck. I am not a duck. I am a Crow."

Everyone laughed again, and the old man kept his posture stoic and face straight, as usual.

Colt laughed now, despite himself. "Yes, I listened when you spoke," he said.

The old Crow looked at Man Killer and indicated Colt, saying, "This one takes very long to finally answer my questions."

Man Killer laughed.

"When I spoke," the warrior said, "what did I call you?"

"I don't know—Colt, I suppose," Chris said.

Charley said, "No, he called you the mighty Colt."

Long-Legged Bear looked at Joshua, saying, "She uses her ears better than him, too."

Long-Legged Bear went on. "Why did I call you the mighty Colt?"

"I don't know," Chris said.

Long-Legged Bear said, "Do you not teach the young ones here to always speak straight?"

"Of course," Colt said.

The Crow said, "Have you not taught them many times to not speak with their tongues forked like the snake?"

"Yes, of course I have!"

"Then why do you not speak straight when I ask you a question?"

Colt said, "I do!"

"You do not."

Colt, angry now, said, "I did, too! What did I lie about?"

Long-Legged Bear said, "What do you think you might have lied about?"

"I don't lie!" Chris yelled.

The old warrior said, "You did. Me ask you why I call you the mighty Colt. You say you do not know, but you do know."

Chris almost kicked the edge of the wooden bench, he was so angry, but he looked at his children and checked himself. Calming down, he smiled softly, while many in the crowd chuckled.

"Okay, you win," he said. "But I wasn't trying to lie. I was trying to be humble. I suppose that some people have called me the mighty Colt because I have had some good things happen that made people think that."

Long-Legged Bear said, "Me, I call you mighty Colt, because you *are* mighty. Man Killer would not ask question about Yost if you had not been mighty Colt once again."

Brenna started giggling and everyone else joined in.

Colt finally said, "Tell you what. Guess I don't ever have to worry about staying humbled. All I have to do is come around here if someone makes a big deal about me. I'll either have a kid sister showing me up, or an old codger driving me crazy."

Joseph grinned and said, "Or two children who will set a good example teaching you how to be honest, Pa."

This remark was so unexpected, it took everybody aback for a second, but ended up bringing the biggest laugh of the day. Chris started chasing his giggling son all over the yard while onlookers laughed. Colt actually slipped and crashed into the wooden bench, which exploded into numerous splinters and slivers of wood. At first, everyone ran to him to see if he was all right.

Once it was discovered he was okay, Long-Legged Bear had everyone on the ground again, saying, "Why do we call him the mighty Colt? He cannot track. He cannot hear. He cannot tell the truth. He cannot even walk after his little boy without knocking apart things around his ranch. Maybe we should call him the Colt Who Is Dumb As A Rock."

Chris sat on the ground and hung his head down, trying hard to hold back his own tears of laughter. While others laughed, Charley came over and grabbed Chris by the arm, yanking him upward. He had accidentally sat down on some spring flowers.

Charley said, "Christopher Columbus Colt, do you know how hard it is to grow those flowers?"

Then Brenna, admiring her bracelet, made everyone smile warmly by saying, "On the Coyote Run Ranch we don't work hard at just growing flowers. We grow heroes, too."